Pearl Tarnor • Carol Levy

לשמואל יחזקאל

מסבתא

לקובי ורעה

מאמא

ושננתם לבניך

"And you shall teach them diligently to your children."

Activities by Roberta Osser Baum, Nina Woldin, Rae Eskin, and Aviva Lucas Gutnick

Editorial consultants: Ellen Rank, Terry Kaye

Special thanks to Danielle Greene for creating the Hebrew files for the revised edition
and to Judy Sandman for proofreading the revised edition.

Artwork by: Joni Levy Liberman (chapter openers); Deborah Zemke (activity art)

Images: Shutterstock: Skellen (cover); LesPalenik (p9); Vera Petrunina (p12); lovelypeace (p17);
Bangun Stock Productions (p21); IgorZD (p26); Rawpixel.com (p30); paul Rushton (p37); 24K-Production (p40);
PeopleImages.com - Yuri A (p43); TamuT (p46); Ruth Black (p49); Alter-ego (p53); fizkes (p56); Africa Studio (p59);
Nina Firsova (p62); Hydras (p66); Maria Kazakova1 (p73); VCoscaron (p76); Alexandra Lande (p80); Rostislav Glinsky (p84);
Nurlan Mammadzada (p88); Shabtay (p91); volcanogirl (p95). Israeli Scouts (p34); Zahava Bogner (p69).

Published by Behrman House, Inc.
Millburn, New Jersey 07041
www.behrmanhouse.com

ISBN 978-1-68115-162-5

Design by Zatar Creative
Revised edition project manager: Aviva Lucas Gutnick
Original edition project manager: Terry Kaye

Printed in China

1 3 5 7 9 8 6 4 2

TABLE OF CONTENTS

ALEF BET page 96

LESSON 1

שַׁבָּת

Shabbat

NEW LETTERS

בּ ת תּ שׁ

NEW VOWELS

◌ַ ◌ָ

BET

1	בַּ	בַּ	בַּ	בַּ	בַּ	בַּ
2	בָּ	בָּ	בָּ	בָּ	בָּ	בָּ
3	בּ	בַּ	בּ	בָּ	בַּ	בּ
4	בַּבַּ	בַּבָּ	בָּבּ	בַּבּ	בַּבָּ	בָּבַּ

SHAPE IT UP

What does ***Bet*** look like?
Close your eyes and picture the letter.
Draw it in the air or use your whole body to make the shape of the letter ***Bet***.

Make up a clue to remember ***Bet***.

What do ◌ַ and ◌ָ sound like?
Make a hand motion to show the shape of ◌ַ and ◌ָ as you say their sound.

I SPY

Read aloud each line.

Find the sound that's different from the others.

Circle it or highlight it.

בּ	בּ	בַּ	בּ	בּ	בּ	1
בָּ	בָּ	בָּ	בּ	בָּ	בָּ	2
בּ	בּ	בּ	בּ	בַּ	בּ	3
בַּ	בַּ	בּ	בַּ	בַּ	בַּ	4

SOUNDS LIKE

Clap your hands as you read aloud each line. Which two Hebrew sounds are the same? Circle them or tell a partner.

בּ	בָּ	בָּ	4	בָּ	בּ	בַּ	1
בּ	בַּ	בּ	5	בּ	בַּ	בּ	2
בַּ	בּ	בָּ	6	בָּ	בָּ	בּ	3

תַּ	תַּ	תָ	תַּ	תָּ	תַ	1
ת	תַ	תָּ	תּ	תָ	תָּ	2

TAV

ת תּ

SHAPE IT UP

What does *Tav* look like? Close your eyes and picture the letter. Draw it in the air or use your whole body to make the shape of the letter *Tav*.

Make up a clue to remember *Tav*.

HEADS UP!

The letters ת and תּ make the same sound.

Say that sound aloud.

I SPY

Read aloud each line.

Find the sound that's different from the others. Jump up and say the name of that letter.

בּ בּ תּ בּ בּ בּ 1

תּ תּ תּ תּ בּ תּ 2

תּ בּ בּ בּ בּ בּ 3

ת ת ת בּ ת ת 4

תּ תּ תּ תּ תּ בּ 5

בּ תּ בּ בּ בּ בּ 6

SHIN

שַׁ שָׁ שׁ שַׁ שָׁ שָׁ 1

שַׁ שָׁ שָׁ שַׁ שׁ שַׁ 2

שַׁשָׁ שָׁשָׁ שָׁשַׁ שָׁשׁ 3

SHAPE IT UP

What does ***Shin*** look like?

Close your eyes and picture the letter. Draw it in the air or use your whole body to make the shape of the letter ***Shin***.

Make up a clue to remember ***Shin***.

READY, SET, READ

Read each line below softly. Read the lines again loudly.

תַּ   בַּ   בּ   תָּ   תַּ   תַּ 1

בָּ   בּ   תּ   תָּ   תַ   בַּ 2

תַּת   תָּתָּ   תָּת   תַּבָּ   תַּבַּ   תַּת 3

תַּבָּ   תַּבּ   בַּת   תַּבַּ   בַּת   תַבּ 4

בַּת   בָּתָּ   תָּבּ   בָּבּ   תַּבּ   בַּת 5

תַּבָּת   בַּתָּת   תַּבָּב   בָּבָּת   בַּבַּת 6

Great job!

EXTRA CREDIT

How many times did you read the Hebrew word for ***daughter***?

_____

I KNOW HEBREW!

Can you find this Hebrew word above?

daughter = בַּת

Read and circle or highlight it.

WORD RIDDLE

I am written on a scroll. I am kept in the Ark. I am read in the synagogue.

My name begins with the letter תּ.

What am I?

I SPY

Read aloud each line.

Find the Hebrew that sounds the same as the English in the box.

Circle it or sing it out loud.

שַׁ	בּ	ת	תַּ	בַּ	שׁ	BAH	1
בּ	תּ	תָּ	שָׁ	שׁ	בָּ	TAH	2
בּ	שָׁ	בָּ	תַּ	שׁ	בַּ	B	3
בַּ	בּ	תַּ	שָׁ	שׁ	תּ	SHAH	4
שׁ	בָּ	תָּ	שׁ	תַ	ת	T	5
שַׁ	שׁ	בּ	תּ	תָּ	שָׁ	SH	6

CONNECTIONS

Connect each Hebrew letter to its name.

What sound does each letter make?

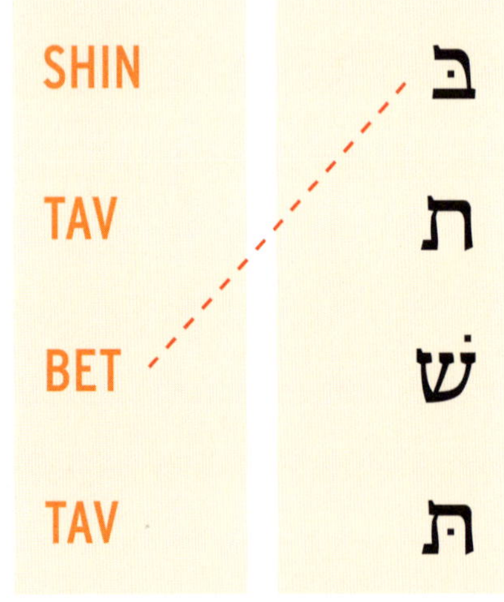

HEADS UP!

Bet (בּ) makes the sound ______.

Tav (תּ or ת) makes the sound ______.

Shin (שׁ) makes the sound ______.

What do you notice about the names of these Hebrew letters and the sounds the letters make?

PICTURE IT IN HEBREW

This cozy בַּיִת is floating in the water. Some people live in a בַּיִת that has wheels, or even built into a mountain. A בַּיִת can have many rooms or just one. The roof of a בַּיִת can be pointed or flat. No matter where your בַּיִת is or how it looks, it is the place you call home.

What do you like best about your בַּיִת?

NEW LETTER בּ

HOUSE – בַּיִת

WELCOMING – שַׁבָּת

On Friday evening when Shabbat begins, we welcome it with blessings and songs.

Circle the objects we use to welcome שַׁבָּת.

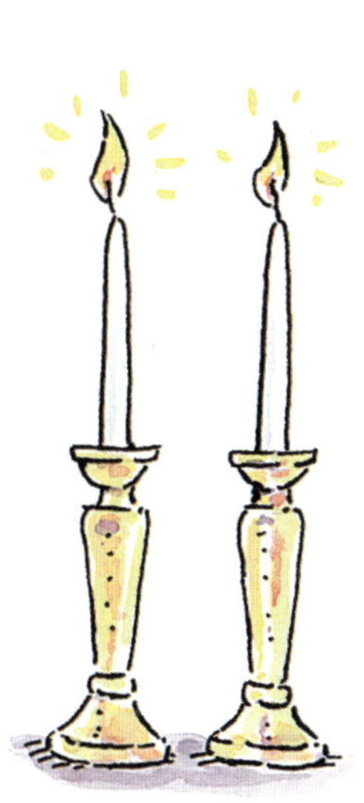

Helper

NEW LETTER

LETTERS YOU KNOW. Say the name and sound of each letter.

בּ ת תּ שׁ

VOWELS YOU KNOW. Say the sound of each vowel.

◌ַ ◌ָ

MEM

מ

1	מַ	מָ	מ	מָ	מ	מַ
2	מַ	בּ	ת	תָּ	מָ	שָׁ
3	מַ	מָ	שׁ	שַׁ	מָ	שׁ

SHAPE IT UP

What does ***Mem*** look like?

Close your eyes and picture the letter.

Draw it in the air or use your whole body to make the shape of the letter ***Mem***.

Make up a clue to remember ***Mem***.

READY, SET, READ

Read the first two lines s-l-o-w-l-y. Read them again correctly as fast as you can.
Take turns with a partner reading every other line at a regular pace.

1 שַׁמָ מָשׁ מַמָ מָשׁ שַׁבָּ בָּת

2 מַשׁ מַבּ מָת מַמַ מַתַּ מַבָּ

3 בַּמַ שָׁמָ תָּמָ בַּת בָּמָ תַמַ

4 מָשַׁב מַתָּשׁ מַבַּת מַמַת בָּמָשׁ

5 תָּמַשׁ שַׁבָּת תַּמַת מַבָּשׁ מָשַׁשׁ

6 שַׁבָּת שַׁמָשׁ מָתָּשׁ מָשַׁשׁ שַׁמָשׁ

7 שַׁמָ שַׁמָשׁ שַׁבָּ שַׁבָּת שַׁמָשׁ

8 שַׁבָּת שַׁמָשׁ שַׁבָּת שַׁמָשׁ שַׁבָּת

I KNOW HEBREW!

Can you find this Hebrew word above?

helper candle on the* hanukkiyah, *the Hanukkah menorah = שַׁמָשׁ

Read it, then circle or point to it each time you find it.

EXTRA CREDIT

How many times did you read the word for ***helper***?

______

PICTURE IT IN HEBREW

There are all kinds of vehicles with wheels, including bicycles, motorcycles, and buses. The red vehicle here is a מְכוֹנִית.

The מְכוֹנִית your family rides in probably has four wheels too.

What do you like best about your מְכוֹנִית?

NEW LETTER

CAR – מְכוֹנִית

CONNECTIONS

Say the sound of each letter.

Match each letter to the picture whose name begins with the same sound.

WORD RIDDLE

You eat me on Passover. I am flat and crunchy. My name begins with the letter מ. What am I?

Draw a picture of me with your favorite topping or tell a partner about your favorite topping for me.

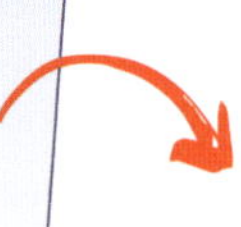

LESSON 3

כַּלָה

Bride

NEW LETTERS

ל כּ ה

LETTERS YOU KNOW. Say the name and sound of each letter.

בּ ת תּ שׁ מ

VOWELS YOU KNOW. Say the sound of each vowel.

ַ ָ

LAMED

1	לַ	לָ	ל	לָ	ל	לַ
2	לָ	לַ	ל	מַ	מָ	מ
3	לָ	בָּ	תַּ	שַׁ	מָ	תָ

SHAPE IT UP

What does ***Lamed*** look like? Close your eyes and picture the letter. Draw it in the air or use your whole body to make the shape of the letter ***Lamed***.

Make up a clue to remember ***Lamed***.

SOUNDS LIKE

Read aloud each word on line 1.

Circle the Hebrew sounds that are the same.

Show a partner and have your partner read them.

Repeat for the other lines.

1	מַשׁ	שַׁמ	מָשָׁ	מָשׁ
2	לָשָׁ	שָׁלָ	שַׁלַ	שַׁל
3	בַּתָ	בַּת	בָּת	תַּב
4	לַבָּ	בַּלָ	לַבּ	לָבַּ
5	לַל	לַמַ	לָמָ	מַל

I SPY

Read aloud each line.

Find and circle the Hebrew that sounds the same as the English in the box.

1	LAH	ל	תַּ	שׁ	לַ	בַּ
2	M	מָ	מ	ת	בּ	ל
3	MAH	שַׁ	בַּ	מַ	תַּ	מ
4	L	ל	שׁ	בּ	לַ	תּ
5	SHAH	שַׁ	בַּ	שׁ	בּ	מַ

KAF

כּ

1	כַּ	כָּ	כּ	כָּ	כַּ	כּ
2	כַּ	בָּ	ל	ת	שַׁ	מַ
3	בָּ	כַּ	ת	בָּ	כַּ	מַ

LETTER BOXES

Say the name of the letter in each box. Circle or point to the sound each letter makes. Say the sound.

Box	Letter	Sounds
1	בּ	B, L, SH, M
2	שׁ	T, SH, M, L
3	מ	T, SH, L, M
4	ת	M, T, SH, B
5	ל	T, M, L, B
6	כּ	H, B, L, K

HAY

ה

הַ הָ ה הַ ה הָ 1

הַ כַּ לָ מָ שַׁ הָ 2

הַ מָ הַ הָ שָׁ הָ 3

SHAPE IT UP

What does ***Hay*** look like?
Close your eyes and picture the letter.
Draw it in the air or use your whole body to make the shape of the letter ***Hay***.

Make up a clue to remember ***Hay***.

HEADS UP!

The letter ה is pronounced "h," but when ה comes at the end of the word and has no vowel under it, it is silent.

READY, SET, READ

Find and read all the sounds and words that start with a ***Hay***. Then read all the sounds and words that end with a ***Hay***. Find and read all the sounds and words that do not have a ***Hay***.

Which sound made you laugh? (Hint: it's on line 2.)

בַּ הָ תָּ הַ כַּ הָ 1

הַל הָבּ הַתּ הָשׁ הָת הַהָ 2

בָּה תָּה שַׁה לָה מַה הַה 3

תָּלָה בָּמָה לָשָׁה כַּמָה שַׁבָּת 4

לָמָה מַכָּה שָׁמָב כַּלָב לָשָׁה 5

הַבַּת הַשַׁמָשׁ הַשַׁבָּת הַמָשָׁל הַכַּלָה 6

כַּלָה הַכַּלָה מַכָּה כַּמָה לָמָה לָשָׁה 7

שַׁבָּת הַכַּלָה שַׁבָּת הַכַּלָה שַׁבָּת הַכַּלָה 8

I KNOW HEBREW!

Can you find these Hebrew words above?

the Sabbath bride = שַׁבָּת הַכַּלָה

bride = כַּלָה

Read and circle or highlight them.

EXTRA CREDIT

How many times did you read the words for ***Sabbath bride***?

_____

PICTURE IT IN HEBREW

You can wear a כּוֹבַע on you head to keep you warm, to protect your face from the sun, or just for fun!

A כּוֹבַע comes in many shapes and sizes and colors.

How do you feel when you wear a כּוֹבַע?

NEW LETTER כּ

HAT – כּוֹבַע

WORD MATCH

Match each Hebrew term with its English meaning. Read each Hebrew-English match aloud.

BRIDE	שַׁבָּת
SABBATH	שַׁמָּשׁ
HELPER	שַׁבָּת הַכַּלָּה
THE SABBATH BRIDE	כַּלָּה

ALEF BET CHART

You know these Hebrew letters:

בּ תּ ת שׁ מ ל כּ ה

Turn to the ***Alef Bet*** chart on page 96. Color in the letters you have learned.

You will return to the chart again after a few more lessons.

The more letters you learn, the more colorful the ***Alef Bet*** chart will become.

LESSON 4

בְּרָכָה

Blessing

LETTERS YOU KNOW. Say the name and sound of each letter.

בּ ת תּ שׁ מ ל כּ ה

VOWELS YOU KNOW. Say the sound of each vowel.

ַ ָ

NEW LETTERS

ר כ

NEW VOWEL

ְ

RESH

ר

1	רַ	רָ	רְ	רְ	רַ	ר
2	בְּ	תְּ	שְׁ	מְ	לְ	כְּ
3	רַ	רְ	בְּ	בַּ	שָׁ	שְׁ

ְ

SHAPE IT UP

What does ***Resh*** look like?
Close your eyes and picture the letter.
Draw it in the air or use your whole body to make the shape of the letter ***Resh***
Make up a clue to remember ***Resh***.

What does ְ sound like?
Make a hand motion to show the shape of ְ as you say its sound.

NAME TAG

Match the Hebrew with its name on each line. Say the sound of each letter.

HAY	TAV	SHIN	תּ	1
SHIN	KAF	BET	בּ	2
RESH	HAY	TAV	ר	3
HAY	SHIN	BET	שׁ	4
KAF	HAY	TAV	ה	5
MEM	SHIN	LAMED	ל	6
LAMED	KAF	BET	כּ	7
MEM	LAMED	TAV	מ	8

CHAF

כְ	כָ	כ	כְ	כָ	כַ	1
כָ	כָּ	כְ	כְּ	כָ	כַּ	2
בַּ	כַ	כָּ	בָּ	כְּ	כְ	3

HEADS UP!

The letters כ and כּ make different sounds.

What sound does כ make?
What sound does כּ make?

Practice making those two sounds.

SHAPE IT UP

What does ***Chaf*** look like?
Close your eyes and picture the letter.

Draw it in the air or use your whole body to make the shape of the letter ***Chaf***.

Make up a clue to help you remember the difference between ***Kaf*** and ***Chaf***.

READY, SET, READ

Read lines 1-4 in a happy 🙂 voice. Read lines 5-8 in a sad 🙁 voice.

1	מָכַ	בָּכָ	כָּכָ	רָכַ	תָּכָ	לְכָ
2	כָה	מָכַ	כָּכָ	כַבָּ	כַּת	כַשְׁ
3	רַכְ	כָּמְ	שַׁכְ	כַּר	תַּכַ	בַּר
4	בָּכָה	כָּכָה	רַכָּה	מָכַר	שָׁכַר	כַּלַת
5	כַּלָה	כָּהָה	כַּמָה	מַכָּה	רָכַשׁ	לַכַּת
6	בָּכַת	כָּכַת	כָּרָה	לְכָה	תָּכָה	לָכַשׁ
7	בָּכְתָה	הַתָּכָה	כָּרַכְתָּ	מָכְרָה	הָלַכְתָּ	
8	הָלַכְתְּ	בְּרָכָה	בְּרָכָה	הָלְכָה	מָשְׁכָה	

I KNOW HEBREW!

Can you find this Hebrew word above?

blessing = בְּרָכָה

How many times did you read the word for ***blessing***?

______

EXTRA CREDIT

Can you find a word above that sounds like another English word for automobile? (Hint: it's on line 3).

What Hebrew letters are in that word?

PICTURE IT IN HEBREW

רֹאשׁ means "head," but רֹאשׁ has other meanings too. רֹאשׁ also means "beginning," like רֹאשׁ הַשָּׁנָה—the beginning of the new year. רֹאשׁ also means "leader," so in Israel, the Prime Minister is called רֹאשׁ הַמֶּמְשָׁלָה—the leader of the government. רֹאשׁ also means "top."

The child here is touching the רֹאשׁ (top) of their רֹאשׁ (head)!

NEW LETTER ר

HEAD – רֹאשׁ

WORDS YOU KNOW

Read each of the words below to a partner. Have your partner say the meaning of the word. Then switch. Do you know the meanings of all the words?

שַׁבָּת שַׁמָּשׁ כַּלָּה בְּרָכָה מַלְכָּה

EXTRA CREDIT

Can you use each Hebrew word in an English sentence?

Example: We welcome שַׁבָּת by lighting candles.

LESSON 5

הַבְדָלָה

Havdalah

Separation

NEW LETTERS

ב ד

NEW VOWEL

◌ֲ

LETTERS YOU KNOW. Say the name and sound of each letter.

בּ ת תּ שׁ מ ל כּ ה ו כ

VOWELS YOU KNOW. Say the sound of each vowel.

◌ַ ◌ָ ◌ְ

VET

◌ֲ

בְ	בַ	בָ	בְ	בָ	בַ	1
בְּ	בְ	בַּ	בַ	הַ	הֲ	2
ב	כ	בְ	כְ	בַ	כַ	3

SHAPE IT UP

What does ***Vet*** look like?
Close your eyes and picture the letter.
Draw it in the air or use your whole body
to make the shape of the letter ***Vet***.

Make up a clue to help you remember
the difference between ***Vet*** and ***Bet***.

What does ◌ֲ sound like?

Make a hand motion to show the
shape of ◌ֲ as you say its sound.

WORD WIZARD

A word you've learned is hidden below.
Cross out the Hebrew letters and vowels that match the English sounds below.
Circle the remaining Hebrew letters and their vowels below to discover the hidden word.

1 SHAH	4 HAH
2 V	5 K
3 LAH	6 T

שַׁ בְּ בְ לָ רָ הָ כָ כְּ ה ת

What does the word mean? ______________________

DALET

ד

דַ דָ דְ דַ דְ ד 1

הֲ רַ דְ רְ כָ דָ 2

דַ רַ דָ רָ ד ר 3

SHAPE IT UP

What does ***Dalet*** look like? Close your eyes and picture the letter.
Draw it in the air or use your whole body to make the shape of the letter ***Dalet***.

Make up a clue to remember ***Dalet***.

READY, SET, READ

Read aloud the odd-numbered lines below in a funny voice.
Read the even-numbered lines in your regular voice.

1 דָד דָר בַּד בַּר דָשׁ רָשׁ

2 דָשׁ דַת דַל דָה דָר דָב

3 מַד כַּד בַּדָ שַׁדָ הַד רַד

4 דָלָה דָבָר דְבַשׁ לָמַד הָדָר דָרָה

5 מָדַד דָשָׁה שָׁדַד דָרַשׁ דָהָה לְבַד

6 הֲמָרָה דְמָמָה הֲלָכָה הֲדָרָה הֲבָרָה

7 כָּתְבָה לָבַשְׁתָּ לָמְדָה דָרַכְתָּ מָדְדָה

8 הַבְדָלָה דְרָשָׁה הֲלָכָה בְּרָכָה הַבְדָלָה

I KNOW HEBREW!

Can you find this Hebrew word above?

havdalah, separation = הַבְדָלָה

Read it and circle or highlight it.

EXTRA CREDIT

How many times did you read the word for ***separation***?

____

SOUNDS LIKE

Read the Hebrew in each box.

Then read the Hebrew on each line. When you hear a sound the same as the sound in the box, snap your fingers.

1	הָבָ	תַבַ	הַבַ	הָרָ
2	בַּד	בָּדְ	בַּרְ	כַּד
3	רָשָׁה	דָשָׁה	רָתָה	רָשַׁ
4	כָּכְ	כַּכְ	בָּבְ	כַּבְ
5	דָבָר	דָבַה	רָבָד	דַבַר

GREEN THUMB

Color the leaf with the Hebrew letter that matches the name in the flower.

PICTURE IT IN HEBREW

You can see a דָג in the sea or in a river. Or maybe you have a דָג in an aquarium at your home, but probably not as large as this דָג!

There's a Bible story we read on Yom Kippur about the prophet Jonah who was swallowed by a big דָג. Jonah tried to run away when God wanted him to teach the people of Nineveh the difference between right and wrong.

Why do you think Jonah ran away?

NEW LETTER ד

FISH – דָג

PICTURE PERFECT

Cirlcethe two objects we can use to welcome שַׁבָּת.

Underline the two objects we can use to say goodbye to שַׁבָּת.

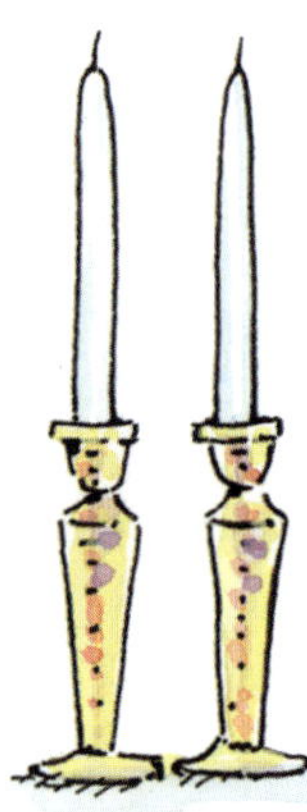

LESSON 6

וְאָהַבְתָּ

And You Shall Love

NEW LETTERS

א ו

LETTERS YOU KNOW. Say the name and sound of each letter.

בּ ת תּ שׁ מ ל כּ ה ר כ ב
ד

VOWELS YOU KNOW. Say the sound of each vowel.

ַ ָ ְ ֲ

1	אַ	אֲ	אָ	אֲ	אָ	אַ
2	אָ	שָׁ	לְ	הֲ	רָ	בְ
3	אֲ	הֲ	אָ	דָ	כְ	רְ

SHAPE IT UP

What does ***Alef*** look like?

Close your eyes and picture the letter.

Draw it in the air or use your whole body to make the shape of the letter ***Alef***.

Make up a clue to remember ***Alef***.

HEADS UP!

The letter א is always silent.
When it has a vowel under it, we say only the vowel sound.

NAME TAG

Read the name of the Hebrew letter in each box. Circle or highlight its matching Hebrew letter. What sound does the letter make?

1	LAMED	מ	ל	ד	ה
2	HAY	ר	ב	ה	ת
3	VET	ב	ד	ת	כ
4	MEM	שׁ	כּ	ל	מ
5	ALEF	ה	ד	ת	א
6	DALET	ה	ד	כ	ר
7	KAF	כּ	תּ	בּ	כ
8	RESH	ד	ב	ר	ת

VAV

#						
1	וָ	וַ	וְ	וְ	וַ	וָ
2	אֲ	דְ	בַ	רְ	כְ	הֲ
3	וָ	וַ	בַ	בְ	רַ	דְ

SHAPE IT UP

What does ***Vav*** look like? Close your eyes and picture the letter.

Draw it in the air or use your whole body to make the shape of the letter ***Vav***.

Make up a clue to remember ***Vav***.

HEADS UP!

The letter ב and ו make the same sound.

What sound do they make?

READY, SET, READ

Read the odd-numbered lines in a funny voice.
Then read the even-numbered lines with an angry voice.

1 דָוַ שָׁוָ תָּוָ שְׁוָ וָלָ וְהָ

2 וָו וָה וַת וַר וַדָ וָאָ

3 לָוָ מַוָ כְּוַ הָוָ תָּו בַּוְ

4 דָוַר שָׁוָה תָּוָה אַוָה לָו אָבָה

5 אֲתַר דָוָה הָוָה שְׁוָא וָלָד דְבַשׁ

6 אֲשָׁרָה אַדְוָה רַאֲוָה וְאַתָּה וְאָהַב

7 אָבְדָה שַׁלְוָה וְאָכַל מְלַוָה הַדָבָר

8 וְהָלַכְתָּ וְאָהַבְתָּ וְאָמַרְתָּ וְלָמַדְתָּ וְאָהַבְתָּ

I KNOW HEBREW!

Can you find this Hebrew word above?

and you shall love = וְאָהַבְתָּ

Read it and circle or highlight it.

EXTRA CREDIT

On what line does וְאָהַבְתָּ appear?

____

PICTURE IT IN HEBREW

Do you have an אָח or אָחוֹת like the siblings in this photo?

The אָח and אָחוֹת here seem to be playing and having fun with each other.

Your אָח or אָחוֹת may play with you, or argue with you—or both! But your אָח or אָחוֹת will always care for you.

NEW LETTER א

BROTHER, SISTER — אָח, אָחוֹת

WORD BUBBLES

With your eyes shut, point to a spot on the page.
Read aloud the word closest to where your finger lands.

Add the number in the circle to your score. Do it three times and see how high you can score.
Play with a partner and see who scores higher.

1 בְּרָכָה	2 הַבְדָלָה	3 הַדָבָר
2 אַהֲבָה	3 וְאָמַרְתָּ	1 וְאָהַב
3 וְאָהַבְתָּ	1 וְאַתָּה	2 אָמְרָה

LESSON 7

צְדָקָה

Justice

LETTERS YOU KNOW. Say the name and sound of each letter.

בּ ת תּ שׁ מ ל כּ ה ר כ ב

ד א ו

VOWELS YOU KNOW. Say the sound of each vowel.

ַ ָ ְ ֲ

NEW LETTERS

ק צ

KOOF

ק

1	קַ	קְ	ק	קָ	קְ	קַ
2	קַ	רַ	כְּ	קְ	כְ	וְ
3	קַ	קְ	כַּ	כְּ	הֲ	אֲ

SHAPE IT UP

What does ***Koof*** look like?
Close your eyes and picture the letter.
Draw it in the air or use your whole body to make the shape of the letter ***Koof***.

Make up a clue to remember ***Koof***.

HEADS UP!

The letters ק and כּ make the same sound.

What sound do they make?

LETTER BOXES

Say the name of the Hebrew letter in each box. Circle or point to the sound each letter makes.

מ	V / M / R
ק	K / CH / L
ה	H / V / T
ל	T / L / SH
ו	V / H / M
ד	R / K / D

TZADEE

צ

1 צַ צְ צָ צ צַ צְ

2 קַ צַ קְ כְּ צְ לְ

3 צַ צְ קַ קְ כְּ דְ

SHAPE IT UP

What does ***Tzadee*** look like?
Close your eyes and picture the letter.

Draw it in the air or use your whole body to make the shape of the letter ***Tzadee***.

Make up a clue to remember ***Tzadee***.

HEADS UP!

The letter ***Tzadee*** makes a special sound.

Say the words ***Matzah Pizza***.

The middle sound in those two words is the sound of ***Tzadee***.

READY, SET, READ

Read lines 1-3 in a strong voice. Read lines 4-6 in a quiet voice. Read lines 7-8 in your regular voice.

צַו	צָב	צַר	צַד	צָה	צָל	1
כְּצַ	בָּצַ	אָצָ	מַצָ	קָצַ	רָצָ	2
אָכָה	צָדַק	כְּצַד	בָּצַר	אָצָה	צָרָה	3
צָבָא	צָבַּר	קָצַר	צְבָת	בָּצָל	מָצָא	4
מַצָה	קְצַת	קַצָב	מַצָב	הַצָב	אָצַר	5
מָצָא	צָלָה	צָמַד	מַצָה	אָצְתָּ	צָמָא	6
וְרָצָה	וְאָצַר	צָרַמְתְּ	צַוָאר	צָוְאָה		7
צְדָקָה	בָּצַרְתָּ	מָצָאתָ	צָדַקְתָּ	צְדָקָה		8

Which words were extra challenging? Practice reading them with a partner.

I KNOW HEBREW!

Can you find the Hebrew word above?

justice = צְדָקָה

Read it and circle or highlight it.

EXTRA CREDIT

Each year at Passover we eat a special food instead of bread.

Find the name of that food above, then read it aloud. What letter is in the middle of the word?

PICTURE IT IN HEBREW

Do you belong to the Boy Scouts or Girl Scouts? In Israel, children participate together in all צוֹפִים activities. Students in every part of Israel join the צוֹפִים. The צוֹפִים have fun together and help their communities.

What symbol do you see on the צוֹפִים uniforms?

NEW LETTER צ

SCOUTS – צוֹפִים

WORD MATCH

Match each Hebrew word with its English meaning. Read each Hebrew-English match aloud.

BLESSING	שַׁמָּשׁ
HELPER	בְּרָכָה
JUSTICE	הַבְדָּלָה
BRIDE	שַׁבָּת
SEPARATION	צְדָקָה
SHABBAT	כַּלָּה

ALEF BET CHART

You have learned eight new letters in Lessons 4-7:

ר כ ב ד א ו ק צ

Turn to the ***Alef Bet*** chart on page 96. Color in the new letters.

How many letters do you now know?
Can you name each letter?

LESSON 8

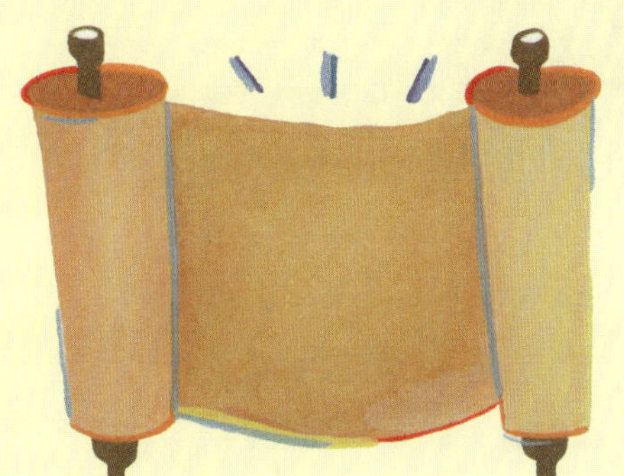

מִצְוָה

Commandment

NEW VOWELS

ִי ִ

LETTERS YOU KNOW. Say the name and sound of each letter.

בּ ת תּ שׁ מ ל כּ ה ר כ ב

ד א ו ק צ

VOWELS YOU KNOW. Say the sound of each vowel.

ִי ִ

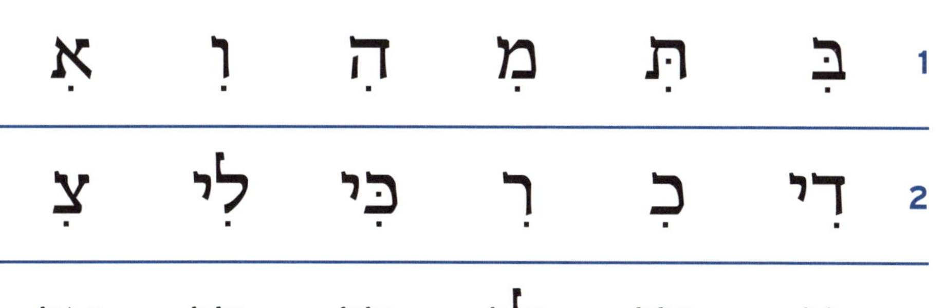

1 בִּ תִּ מִ הִ וִ אִ

2 דִי כִ רִ כִּי לִי צִ

3 וִי מִי לִי כִּי בִּי אִי

Which Hebrew sound reminds you of a buzzing insect?
Circle or highlight it above.

SHAPE IT UP

What does ִ sound like?
Make a hand motion to show the shape of ִ as you say its sound.

What does ִי sound like?
Make a hand motion to show the shape of ִי as you say its sound.

READY, SET, READ

Read lines 1-4. Then, take a break. Stand up and stretch your body. Read lines 5-8.

1 מִקְ צַדִי לְבִי אֲוִי דָוִ בְּרִי

2 שִׁשָׁה הִכָּה בִּיב שְׁמִי צִיר הֲכִי

3 הִיא אִישׁ אִשָׁה אִמָא בְּכִי בְּלִי

4 רַבִּי אֲוִיר דָוִד בִּימָה דָתִי תִּיק

5 שִׁירָה תִּירָא רִמָה קְרִיאַת לְבִיבָה קָצִיר

6 צַדִיק בְּרִיאַת קַדִישׁ אָבִיב קְהִלָה מִקְרָא

7 צִיצִית בְּרִית מִילָה תִּקְוָה הַתִּקְוָה

8 מִצְוָה הַמִצְוָה בַּר מִצְוָה בַּת מִצְוָה

I KNOW HEBREW!

Can you find the Hebrew words above?
Read and circle or highlight them.

knotted fringes on the corners of the tallit = צִיצִית

Kaddish = קַדִישׁ

"The Hope", the national anthem of Israel = הַתִּקְוָה

commandment = מִצְוָה

bar mitzvah = בַּר מִצְוָה

bat mitzvah = בַּת מִצְוָה

Mommy = אִמָא

PICTURE IT IN HEBREW

You can make and listen to מוּסִיקָה almost anywhere in the world. מוּסִיקָה can wake you up or calm you down. מוּסִיקָה can also inspire you.

This musician is making מוּסִיקָה on a traveling piano!

What kind of מוּסִיקָה do you enjoy? How does it make you feel?

NEW VOWEL

MUSIC – מוּסִיקָה

WORD WIZARD

Read aloud each line.

Find the Hebrew letter that is found in every word on the line.

Write the name of the letter on the line.

1 מַלְבִּיש רַבִּי מִדְבָּר דִּבְּרָה

2 אִירָא בְּקִרְבִּי בְּרִית מִדְרָשׁ

3 תָּמִיד מָרָה בִּימָה אָמַרְתִּי

4 מַצִּיל צְדָקָה צִיצִית מִצְוָה

5 הַתִּקְוָה אָבִיו צִוָּה בְּשַׁלְוִי

6 לְהָבִיא אִשָּׁה אָהַבְתִּי קְהִילָּה

LESSON 9

שְׁמַע

Hear

NEW LETTER

ע

LETTERS YOU KNOW. Say the name and sound of each letter.

בּ ת תּ שׁ מ ל כּ ה ר כ ב

ד א ו ק צ

VOWELS YOU KNOW. Say the sound of each vowel.

ַ ָ ְ ֲ ִ ִי

AYIN

1	עַ	עָ	עֲ	עִ	עִי	עָ
2	עַ	אֲ	הַ	עֲ	אֲ	הֲ
3	עִי	צִי	קִי	אֲ	הֲ	עֲ

SHAPE IT UP

What does ***Ayin*** look like?
Close your eyes and picture the letter.

Draw it in the air or use your whole body to make the shape of the letter ***Ayin***.

Make up a clue to remember ***Ayin***.

HEADS UP!

The letter ע does not have its own sound.

When it has a vowel under it, we say only the vowel sound.

What other letter doesn't have its own sound?

READY, SET, READ

Read line 1 softly, then read line 2 loudly. Continue alternating how you read each line. Then read the lines again, this time reading the odd-numbered lines loudly and the even-numbered lines softly.

1 עָשִׂי עָתִי עַב צָעִי מַע דַע

2 עַל עָב עַד רַע עִיר עַר

3 וַעַד דַעַת עַתָּה רַעַשׁ בַּעַל עָבַר

4 שְׁמַע רָעָב צָעִיר תָּקַע עִמָה שָׁעָה

5 רָקִיעַ עָתִיד עָשִׁיר אַרְבַּע עַתִיק עִבְרִי

6 עִבְרִית מַעֲרִיב תְּקִיעָה עֲמִידָה קְעָרָה

7 שַׁעֲוָה עָבַדְתִּי שִׁבְעָה עֲתִיקָה עֲמִידָה

8 שְׁמַע תִּשְׁמַע שְׁמִיעָה קְרִיאַת שְׁמַע

I KNOW HEBREW!

Can you find this Hebrew word above?

hear = שְׁמַע

Read it loudly so that others can ***hear*** you.

Can you find this Hebrew word above?

Hebrew = עִבְרִית

What letter does it start with?

What letter does it end with?

PICTURE IT IN HEBREW

This photo of the עוֹלָם was taken from outer space.

Looking at the עוֹלָם from this distance, it's easy to imagine everyone coming together to work for תִּיקּוּן עוֹלָם —caring for the environment and all living things.

How can you take care of the עוֹלָם?

NEW LETTER ע

WORLD – עוֹלָם

DRUM BEAT

Draw a drumstick on each drum whose letter makes a sound.

How many drumsticks did you draw? ________ What is the name of the letter? ________

TIC-TAC-TOE

Play tic-tac-toe with a partner. Read the sounds correctly to make an X or an O.

רָ	מְ	הִי
בָ	דִ	כַ
עַ	צִ	אָ

עָ	כַ	תְ
וָ	הֱ	צִי
רִ	בְּ	קִ

בָּ	תִי	קַ
לְ	אֱ	כִ
שַׁ	עַ	וִי

Prophet

NEW LETTERS

נ ן

LETTERS YOU KNOW. Say the name and sound of each letter.

בּ ת תּ שׁ מ ל כּ ה ר כ ב

ד א ו ק צ ע

VOWELS YOU KNOW. Say the sound of each vowel.

ַ ָ ְ ֲ ִ ִי

FINAL NUN/NUN

ן נ

1	נַ	נָ	נִי	נְ	נִ	נְ
2	נִ	נִי	עִי	וִי	רִ	בִ
3	לָן	דָן	מִין	רָן	מִן	כַּן

Which Hebrew sound reminds you of a part of your body?

SHAPE IT UP

What do ***Nun*** and ***Final Nun*** look like?

Close your eyes and picture the letters.

Draw them in the air or use your whole body to make the shapes of the letters ***Nun*** and ***Final Nun***.

Make up clues to remember ***Nun*** and ***Final Nun***.

HEADS UP!

There are five letters of the Hebrew alphabet that have a different form when they come at the end of a word.

When a נ comes at the end of a word, it is a ***Final*** ן.

READY, SET, READ

Read lines 1-3 in a happy 🙂 voice. Read lines 4-5 in a sad 🙁 voice.
Read lines 6-8 in your regular voice.

1 נָן נָו נְעִי קַן בִּין

2 נִין לָן דָן מָן שִׁין רָן

3 דִין בְּנִי עָנִי נָקִי אֲנִי נָא

4 שָׁנָה לָבָן עָנָו רִנָה עָנַד נַעַר

5 נָבִיא בִּינָה נְשָׁמָה מִשְׁנָה נְעָרָה

6 מַאֲמִין שְׁכִינָה כַּוָנָה נְעִילָה מַרְבִּין

7 רַעֲנָן מִשְׁכָּן לְהָבִין קַנְקַן לַמְדָן

8 נָבִיא מְדִינָה מַה נִשְׁתַּנָה נָבִיא

I KNOW HEBREW!

Can you find the Hebrew word above?

prophet = נָבִיא

Read it and circle or highlight it.

EXTRA CREDIT

At the Passover seder, the youngest child asks the Four Questions.

Can you find the two Hebrew words in the lines above that introduce the Four Questions? Read them.

If you remember the tune to the Four Questions, sing the first line!

PICTURE IT IN HEBREW

Giving someone a נְשִׁיקָה can mean many things, such as, "Hi, I'm happy to see you," or "Goodbye, I'll miss you!" What do you think this boy's נְשִׁיקָה on his father's cheek means?

On Shabbat, when the Torah is caried around the synagogue sanctuary, people in the congregation give the Torah a נְשִׁיקָה. This is one way to show they cherish the Torah.

Can you think of another Jewish object people touch and give a נְשִׁיקָה?

NEW LETTER נ

KISS – נְשִׁיקָה

WORD POWER

Read aloud the Hebrew words on each line.
Circle or highlight the word that has the same meaning as the English in the box.

1	HEBREW	שָׁנָה	עִבְרִית	כַּוָּנָה	קְרִיאַת
2	PROPHET	שְׁכִינָה	מַעֲרִיב	אַרְבַּע	נָבִיא
3	AND YOU SHALL LOVE	נְשָׁמָה	תְּקִיעָה	וְאָהַבְתָּ	בְּרִית
4	COMMANDMENT	קַדִּישׁ	אִמָּא	אַהֲבָה	מִצְוָה
5	THE HOPE	קַבָּלַת	הַתִּקְוָה	מִשְׁכַּן	נְעִילָה

LESSON 11

Braided Bread

for Shabbat and holidays

LETTERS YOU KNOW. Say the name and sound of each letter.

בּ ת תּ שׁ מ ל כּ ה ר כ ב

ד א ו ק צ ע נ ן

VOWELS YOU KNOW. Say the sound of each vowel.

ַ ָ ְ ֲ ִ ִי

NEW LETTER

CHET

1	חַ	חִ	חִי	חֲ	חָ	ח
2	כַ	חַ	כִי	חִי	כָ	חָ
3	חִי	הִי	חֲ	הֲ	חָ	הָ

SHAPE IT UP

What does ***Chet*** look like?
Close your eyes and picture the letter.

Draw it in the air or use your whole body to make the shape of the letter ***Chet***.

Make up a clue to remember ***Chet***.

HEADS UP!

The letters ח and כ make the same sound.

What sound do these letters make?

READY, SET, READ

Read all the words that start with ***Chet***, and have a partner read all the words that end with ***Chet***. Together read the words that have ***Chet*** in the middle. Then whisper the words that do not have a ***Chet***.

1 חִכָּ חָבִי חָתָ בָּח אַח צָח

2 חָל חִיל חַד חָשׁ חִישׁ חִימִי

3 קַח צַח נָח לָח אָח חַוָה

4 חִכָּה שָׁכַח חָבִיב חֲבָל חָתָן לָקַח

5 חַלָה חָלִיל וְצָחַק אַחַת חָצִיר חָנָן

6 מִנְחָה חֲמִשָׁה שָׁלְחָה חִירִיק בָּחַרְתָּ

7 רַחֲמָן הָרַחֲמָן שַׁחֲרִית חֲתִימָה חֲדָשָׁה

8 הַחַלָה הַבְּרָכָה חַלָה לְשַׁבָּת הָרַחֲמָן

I KNOW HEBREW!

Can you find these Hebrew words above?

the Merciful One (God) = הָרַחֲמָן

braided bread = חַלָה

Read and circle or highlight them.

EXTRA CREDIT

How many times did you read the word for ***braided bread***?

PICTURE IT IN HEBREW

You can buy almost anything at a חֲנוּת.

This חֲנוּת in Israel sells all kinds of snacks and food and drinks.

Which of the foods in this חֲנוּת do you like?

LETTER AND VOWEL WORKOUT

You have learned all these letters and vowels! Say the name of each letter in lines 1-8. Take turns with a partner reading all the lines. As you do, choose a movement for each line. For example, scratch your head while reading line 1, or rub your hands together while reading line 2.

SOUNDS LIKE

Can you find the Hebrew that sounds like the English word for:

- A hot beverage?
- Something you use to open a lock?
- A buzzing insect?

Circle or highlight those sounds.

אִי	אִ	אֲ	אָ	אַ	1
בִּי	בִּ	בְּ	בָּ	בַּ	2
בִי	בִ	בְ	בָ	בַ	3
דִי	דִ	דְ	דָ	דַ	4
הִי	הִ	הֲ	הָ	הַ	5
חִי	חִ	חֲ	חָ	חַ	6
כִּי	כִּ	כְּ	כָּ	כַּ	7
תִי	תִ	תְ	תָ	תַ	8

עֲלִיָה

Going Up

the honor of being called up to recite the blessings over the Torah

LETTERS YOU KNOW. Say the name and sound of each letter.

בּ ת תּ שׁ מ ל כּ ה ר כ ב

ד א ו ק צ ע נ ן ח

VOWELS YOU KNOW. Say the sound of each vowel.

◌ַ ◌ָ ◌ְ ◌ֲ ◌ִ ◌ִי

NEW LETTER

י

YUD

1	יַ	יָ	יִי	יִ	יְ	יָ
2	יַ	וַ	יְ	וְ	יִי	וִי
3	יָשָׁ	יָר	יִן	יְשִׁי	חַי	יְדִי

SHAPE IT UP

What does ***Yud*** look like? Close your eyes and picture the letter.

Draw it in the air or use your whole body to make the shape of the letter ***Yud***.

Make up a clue to remember ***Yud***.

READY, SET, READ

Read aloud the lines below while standing on one foot. Switch to the other foot halfway.

1 יָד יְהִי יַיִן יַמִי יָדִי יָמָה

2 שַׁיִשׁ יָשָׁן מִיָד נְיָר לַיִל הֲיִי

3 בַּיִת יָשָׁר יַעַר חַיָה עַיִן יָשַׁב

4 יָדַע אַיִל חַיָב יָחִיד יָקָר מַעְיָן

5 יְצִיר הָיָה יָוָן חַיִל יָצָא עֲדַיִן

6 יַחְדָו יִרְאָה יִצְחָק יַבָּשָׁה צִיַרְתִּי

7 עֲלִיָה כְּוִיָה יִוָכַח יַלְדָה יְדִיעָה

8 יְשִׁיבָה יִשְׁתַּבַח הָיְתָה מִנְיָן עֲלִיָה

I KNOW HEBREW!

Can you find these Hebrew words above?

***aliyah*, going up** = עֲלִיָה

***minyan*, ten Jewish adults, the minimum needed to recite some prayers** = מִנְיָן

Read and circle or highlight them.

EXTRA CREDIT

Can you find the word יָד above?

It is the Hebrew word for ***hand***.

It is also the word for the pointer used to touch the parchment of the Torah.

PICTURE IT IN HEBREW

Anyone can celebrate your יוֹם הוּלֶדֶת with a cake and party hat!

In Israel, it's custom to lift up the person celebrating their יוֹם הוּלֶדֶת in a chair while everyone sings "הַיּוֹם הוּלֶדֶת," which means "Today is the birthday."

When is your יוֹם הוּלֶדֶת?

CONNECTIONS

Read the word parts in each column.

Connect the beginning of a word in the right column to its ending in the left column.

Read each word aloud.

וָה	שַׁ	1
הַבְתָּ	הַבְ	2
יָן	בְּרָ	3
דָלָה	וְאָ	4
בָּת	צְדָ	5
יָה	מִצְ	6
קָה	מִנְ	7
כָּה	עֲלִ	8

To Life

LETTERS YOU KNOW. Say the name and sound of each letter.

בּ ת תּ שׁ מ ל כּ ה ר כ ב

ד א ו ק צ ע נ ן ח י

VOWELS YOU KNOW. Say the sound of each vowel.

◌ַ ◌ָ ◌ְ ◌ֲ ◌ִ ◌ִ ◌ִי

NEW LETTER

ם

FINAL MEM

ם

1	תָּם	קָם	צָם	דָם	אִם	חַם
2	עַם	שָׁם	יָם	בָּם	רָם	עִם
3	יִם	תִּים	רַיִם	לִים	הָם	אִים

SHAPE IT UP

What does ***Final Mem*** look like?
Close your eyes and picture the letter.

Draw it in the air or use your whole body to make the shape of the letter ***Final Mem***.

Make up a clue to remember ***Final Mem***.

HEADS UP!

There are five letters in the Hebrew alphabet that have a different form when they come at the end of a word.

When a מ comes at the end of a word, it is a ***Final*** ם.

What other letter have you learned that has a different form at the end of a word?

READY, SET, READ

Read aloud each line. When you read a word that ends in the sound "eem," stand up. When you read a word that ends in "ahm," sit down.

1 הָלַם אַחִים עָלִים מִרְיָם בַּדִים תָּרַם

2 אִיִם שְׁנַיִם בָּתִים אָדָם דַקִים מִצְרַיִם

3 חָכָם רַעַם יָמִים רַבִּים חַיִים דָמַם

4 בָּנִים מַיִם אָדָם שְׁתַּיִם מִלִים אָשָׁם

5 נָשִׁים שָׁמַיִם דְבָרִים יָדַיִם קָמִים עָלִים

6 אַבְרָהָם נְבִיאִים כְּרָמִים שִׁבְעִים אֲנָשִׁים

7 עִבְרִים רַחֲמִים יְלָדִים צַדִיקִים מְלָכִים

8 עֲבָדִים יְצִיאַת מִצְרַיִם לְחַיִים לְחַיִים

I KNOW HEBREW!

Can you find these Hebrew words above?

to life = לְחַיִים

the name of the first human in the Torah = אָדָם

the Exodus, going out from Egypt = יְצִיאַת מִצְרַיִם

Read and circle or highlight them.

WORD BUBBLES

With your eyes shut, point to a spot on the page. Read the word closest to where your finger lands.

Add the number in the circle to your score. Do it three times and see how high you can score. Play with a partner and see who scores higher.

Want a higher score? Earn one point for each word translated correctly.

VOCABULARY CHALLENGE

You know the English meaning of many of the words in the ***Word Bubbles*** activity above. Read the Hebrew and give the English meaning for the words you know.

PICTURE IT IN HEBREW

Every living thing on earth needs מַיִם.

Plants need מַיִם to grow, fish need מַיִם to live in. מַיִם also keeps us clean. The expression מַיִם לְחַיִּים means "water for life," and reminds us how precious מַיִם is, especially in Israel and other deserts, where very little rain falls.

Can you think of something else that water is used for?

NEW LETTER ם

WATER – מַיִם

WORD POWER

Read aloud the Hebrew words on each line.
Circle or highlight the word that has the same meaning as the English in the box.

1	BLESSING	בְּרָכָה	חַלָּה	הַבְדָּלָה	שַׁמָּשׁ
2	TO LIFE	מִצְוָה	חָכָם	עֲבָדִים	לַחַיִּים
3	HEAR	נָבִיא	בָּנִים	שְׁמַע	שְׁתַּיִם
4	GOING UP	מִצְרַיִם	עֲלִיָּה	עַיִן	יְצִיאַת
5	JUSTICE	יְלָדִים	שָׁמַיִם	צְדָקָה	יְשִׁיבָה

ALEF BET CHART

You have learned six new letters in Lessons 9-13:

ע נ ן ח י ם

Turn to the ***Alef Bet*** chart on page 96. Color in the new letters.
Can you say the name and sound of each letter you now know?

LESSON 14

תּוֹרָה

Torah, Teaching

NEW VOWELS

וֹ ˙

LETTERS YOU KNOW. Say the name and sound of each letter.

בּ ת תּ שׁ מ ל כּ ה ר כ ב

ד א ו ק צ ע נ ן ח י ם

VOWELS YOU KNOW. Say the sound of each vowel.

ַ ָ ְ ֲ ִ ֵ י

וֹ ˙

1 תּוֹ בּוֹ רוֹ מוֹ לוֹ דוֹ נוֹ

2 אֹ צֹ קֹ עֹ נֹ חֹ יֹ

3 מֹעַ עוֹת אָנֹ שׁוֹן קֹב דוֹשׁ

SHAPE IT UP

What does וֹ sound like? Make a hand motion to show the shape of וֹ as you say its sound.

What does ˙ sound like? Make a hand motion to show the shape of ˙ as you say its sound.

Look at lines 1-3 above. What sounds like:

The opposite of "yes"? Circle or highlight it.

The opposite of "high"? Circle or highlight it.

HEADS UP!

Usually a vowel is found below a letter: רִ, שַׁ.

But the vowel וֹ or ˙ comes after a letter: תּוֹ מֹ.

READY, SET, READ

Read aloud the odd-numbered lines. Read aloud the even-numbered lines.

1 כֹּל לֹא אוֹת יוֹם חוֹל צֹאן

2 עוֹד קוֹל מוֹת שׁוֹר צוֹם חוֹר

3 שָׁמַע יָבֹא אֹתָם דָתוֹ אָנֹכִי כְּמוֹ

4 אָבוֹת מְאֹד כָּבוֹד לָשׁוֹן נָכוֹן שָׁעוֹת

5 קָדוֹשׁ תּוֹרָה צִיוֹן מוֹרָה תְּהֹם מְלֹא

6 שְׁלֹמֹה אַהֲרֹן יַעֲקֹב אֲדוֹן עוֹלָם

7 הַמּוֹצִיא שַׁבָּת שָׁלוֹם רֹאשׁ הַשָּׁנָה

8 תּוֹרָה בְּרָכוֹת מִצְווֹת דּוֹרוֹת כֹּהֲנִים

How did you do? Choose four words that were challenging to read. Read them again to a partner.

I KNOW HEBREW!

Can you find these Hebrew words above?
Circle or point to them. Then read each word.

Torah, teaching =
תּוֹרָה

Holy =
קָדוֹשׁ

Hello, goodbye, peace =
שָׁלוֹם

A peaceful Shabbat =
שַׁבָּת שָׁלוֹם

Blessing over bread =
הַמּוֹצִיא

Jewish New Year =
רֹאשׁ הַשָּׁנָה

EXTRA CREDIT

Can you find the name of the ***Jewish New Year*** in the words above?

Circle or highlight it.

Can you recite the בְּרָכָה we say over חַלָּה?

PICTURE IT IN HEBREW

When a תִינוֹק is born, everyone celebrates!

A תִינוֹק is welcomed into the Jewish community with a special ceremony to receive its Hebrew name.

What is your Hebrew name?

BABY – תִינוֹק

CONNECTIONS

Read the word in each column.

Connect each word in column א with a word in column בּ to make a phrase.

Say the phrase out loud.

א	בּ
שַׁבָּת	נִשְׁתַּנָּה
מַה	מִצְוָה
רֹאשׁ	שָׁלוֹם
יְצִיאַת	הַשָּׁנָה
בַּת	מִצְרָיִם

LESSON 15

טַלִּית

Tallit,
Prayer Shawl

NEW LETTER

ט

LETTERS YOU KNOW. Say the name and sound of each letter.

בּ ת תּ שׁ מ ל כּ ה ר כ ב

ד א ו ק צ ע נ ן ח י ם

VOWELS YOU KNOW. Say the sound of each vowel.

◌ַ ◌ָ ◌ְ ◌ֲ ◌ִ ◌ִי ◌וֹ

◌ֹ

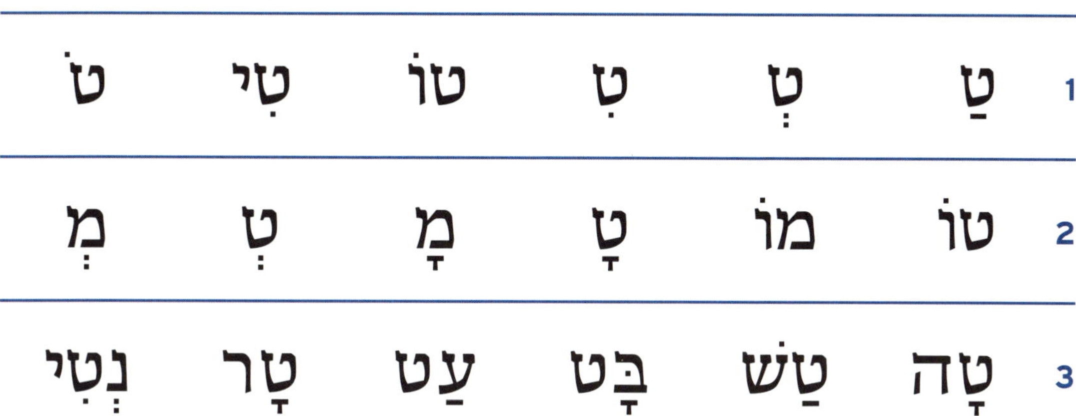

1 טַ טְ טִ טוֹ טִי טֹ

2 טוֹ מוֹ טָ מָ טְ מְ

3 טָה טַשׁ בָּט עַט טָר נְטִי

TET

SHAPE IT UP

What does *Tet* look like?

Close your eyes and picture the letter.

Draw it in the air or use your whole body to make the shape of the letter ***Tet***.

Make up a clue to remember ***Tet***.

HEADS UP!

The letters תּ, ת, and ט make the same sound. What sound do they make?

READY, SET, READ

Read aloud all the words that begin with ***Tet***. Find all the words that end with ***Tet*** and read those too. Then read all the words that neither start nor end with ***Tet***.

1	טוֹן	טִיב	מָט	אַט	חַיָט	מוֹטוֹ
2	טוֹב	טַל	אִטִי	טָרִי	שׁוֹט	קָט
3	מִטָה	מוֹט	קָטָן	חִטָה	שָׁחַט	לָטַשׁ
4	לְאַט	מָטָר	חָטָא	מְעַט	שְׁבָט	בָּטַח
5	טַלִית	טָהוֹר	אָטָד	טַעַם	טִבְעִי	טָמַן
6	קְטַנָה	עֲטָרָה	מִקְלָט	חֲטָאִים	הִבִּיטָה	
7	שְׁבָטִים	טוֹבִים	בִּטָחוֹן	נְטִילַת	יָדַיִם	
8	טַלִית	שָׁנָה	טוֹבָה	יוֹם	טוֹב	

Great job!

I KNOW HEBREW!

Can you find these words above?

tallit, prayer shawl = טַלִית

holiday, festival = יוֹם טוֹב

Happy New Year = שָׁנָה טוֹבָה

On what Jewish holiday would you say שָׁנָה טוֹבָה?

Read and circle or highlight them.

PICTURE IT IN HEBREW

Did you know that in Hebrew, letters are written from right to left, but numbers on a טֶלֶפוֹן are written from left to right?

Who do you like to talk to on a טֶלֶפוֹן?

NEW LETTER ט

TELEPHONE – טֶלֶפוֹן

SHOW WHAT YOU KNOW

Connect each Hebrew word with its English meaning.

BLESSING	צְדָקָה
PRAYER SHAWL	שַׁבָּת
JUSTICE	בְּרָכָה
SHABBAT	טַלִּית

TORAH	הַבְדָּלָה
GOING UP	בַּת
SEPARATION	תּוֹרָה
DAUGHTER	עֲלִיָּה

HOLY	שְׁמַע
TO LIFE	וְאָהַבְתָּ
HEAR	לְחַיִּים
AND YOU SHALL LOVE	קָדוֹשׁ

PROPHET	מִצְוָה
BRAIDED BREAD	שַׁמָּשׁ
HELPER	נָבִיא
COMMANDMENT	חַלָּה

אֱמֶת

Truth

NEW VOWELS

◌ֱ ◌ֶ

LETTERS YOU KNOW. Say the name and sound of each letter.

בּ ת תּ שׁ מ ל כּ ה ר כ ב

ד א ו ק צ ע נ ן ח י ם

ט

VOWELS YOU KNOW. Say the sound of each vowel.

◌ַ ◌ָ ◌ְ ◌ֲ ◌ִ ◌ִי ◌וֹ

◌ֹ

1	דֶ	בֶּ	תֶ	טֶ	אֱ	יֶ
2	שֶׁ	עֱ	מֶ	לֶ	קֶ	צֶ
3	תֶּם	עֶד	רֶב	חֱלִי	דֶשׁ	יֶה

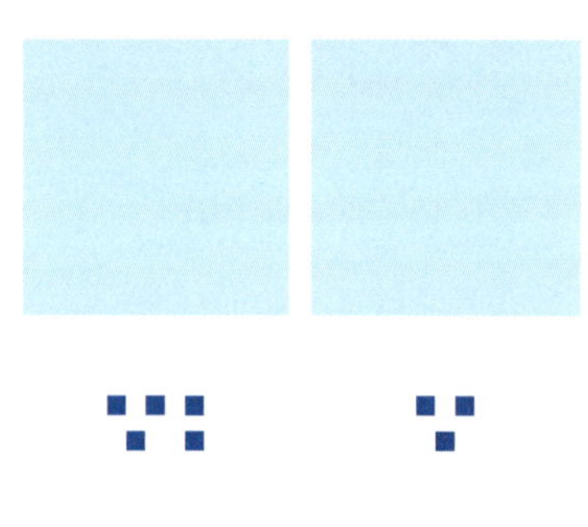

SHAPE IT UP

What does ◌ֶ sound like? Make a hand motion to show the shape of ◌ֶ as you say its sound.

What does ◌ֱ sound like? Make a hand motion to show the shape of ◌ֱ as you say its sound.

READY, SET, READ

Choose two lines for a partner to read aloud. Then have your partner choose two lines for you to read. Continue until you've each read every line on the page.

1 אֶת אֶל שֶׁלִי שֶׁלֹא אֱמֶת אַתֶּן

2 אֲשֶׁר שֶׁמֶשׁ יֶלֶד לָכֶם אֹהֶל אֶבֶן

3 אַתֶּם נֶצַח חֹדֶשׁ כֹּתֶל טֶרֶם אֶחָד

4 רוֹצֶה שֶׁבַע עֶרֶב מוֹרֶה נֶאֱמָן שְׁמוֹנֶה

5 וְנֶאֱמַר מְחַיֶּה רוֹעֶה עוֹלֶה הֶחֱלִיט יִהְיֶה

6 לְעוֹלָם וָעֶד תּוֹרַת אֱמֶת מִצְוָה אֶתְכֶם

7 אֲרוֹן הַקֹּדֶשׁ כֶּתֶר תּוֹרָה וַיֹּאמֶר אֱלֹהִים

8 אֱלֹהִים הַמּוֹצִיא לֶחֶם אֱמֶת וְצֶדֶק

I KNOW HEBREW!

Can you find these Hebrew words above?

truth = אֱמֶת

God = אֱלֹהִים

Who brings forth bread = הַמּוֹצִיא לֶחֶם

the Holy Ark = אֲרוֹן הַקֹּדֶשׁ

Read and circle or highlight them.

EXTRA CREDIT

Circle the first letter in the Hebrew word for truth?

Say the name of the letter.

How many other words above start with that letter? ___

PICTURE IT IN HEBREW

Sweet oranges and bright red cherry tomatoes grow in Israel.

Another kind of אֹכֶל people eat in Israel is hummus, a delicious dip made from chickpeas.

Falafel, the round balls in the picture, are also made from chickpeas. Yum!

What kind of אֹכֶל do you like to eat?

FOOD – אֹכֶל

SHOW WHO YOU KNOW

Match each Hebrew name with its translation. Read each match aloud. Do you know anyone with those names?

MIRIAM	חַנָה	MOSES	אָדָם
REBECCA	דְבוֹרָה	BENJAMIN	מֹשֶׁה
HANNAH	רִבְקָה	ADAM	דָוִד
DEBORAH	מִרְיָם	DAVID	בִּנְיָמִן

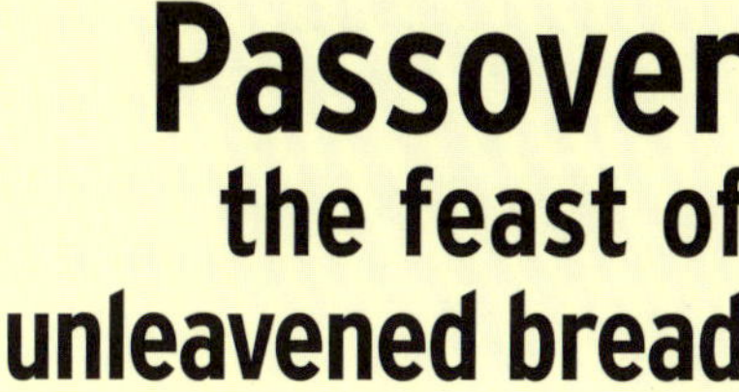

LETTERS YOU KNOW. Say the name and sound of each letter.

בּ ת תּ שׁ מ ל כּ ה ר כ ב

ד א ו ק צ ע נ ן ח י ם

ט

VOWELS YOU KNOW. Say the sound of each vowel.

◌ַ ◌ָ ◌ְ ◌ֲ ◌ִ ◌ִי ◌וֹ

◌ֹ ◌ֶ ◌ֱ

NEW LETTER

ס

PAY

1	פּוֹ	פֶּ	פַּ	פְּ	פֹּ	פָּ
2	פֶּה	פְּרִי	פֹּה	פֶּן	פַּת	פֶּתִי
3	פְּשָׁ	פֶּשַׁ	צִפּוֹ	כַּפִּי	טִפָּ	פֶּרֶ

Which word above sounds like something you write with? Write it in Hebrew here: ____________

SHAPE IT UP

What does ***Pay*** look like? Close your eyes and picture the letter.
Draw it in the air or use your whole body to make the shape of the letter ***Pay***.

Make up a clue to remember ***Pay***.

RHYME TIME

Read aloud the words to the right. Find the two rhyming words on each line. Circle them or read them to a partner.

1	נוֹרָא	צוֹם	תּוֹרָה	אוֹת
2	יוֹרָם	מוֹצִיא	הוֹצִיא	הוֹלְכִים
3	תֶּרֶק	לֶחֶם	כֶּתֶר	רֶחֶם
4	פֶּרֶק	טִפָּה	פֶּרַח	כִּפָּה
5	טָהוֹר	טַלִית	מִטָה	שָׁחוֹר
6	פִּדְיוֹן	פְּעָמִים	פִּתְאֹם	עִפָּרוֹן

1	סַ	סִ	סִי	סוֹ	סֹ	סֶ
2	סַל	סַע	סֶלָה	סָב	סַם	סִיר
3	חַסְ	יְסוֹ	סִיוָ	סַבְ	מִסְ	נַסֶ

SHAPE IT UP

What does ***Samech*** look like?

Close your eyes and picture the letter.

Draw it in the air or use your whole body to make the shape of the letter ***Samech***.

Make up a clue to remember ***Samech***.

READY, SET, READ

Read aloud the first word on every line. Next, read the second word on every line.
Then take a minute to stretch or walk around the room. Now you're ready to read more!
Practice reading aloud the words you haven't read yet.

1 כּוֹס סֶלַע מַס פֶּסַח סְתָו סִיוָן

2 סְתָם חֶסֶד סַבָּא סָבְתָּא חֲסִיד כַּסְפּוֹ

3 נִיסָן סִדְרָה חַסְדוֹ סַנְדָק יְסוֹד מִסְפָּר

4 מָסֹרֶת נִסִים נִכְנָס כְּסוֹד מְנַסֶּה לַעֲסֹק

5 סְבִיבוֹן מִסָבִיב בָּסִיס הִסְפִּיד וְנִסְכּוֹ מַחְסִי

6 מְסַפֶּרֶת כְּנֶסֶת נִסְפָּח הַכְנָסַת מַסְפִּיק

7 חֲסָדִים חֲסִידִים פַּרְנָסָה סְלִיחָה סְלִיחוֹת

8 פֶּסַח כַּרְפַּס חֲרוֹסֶת מַצָה מָרוֹר פֶּסַח

Were any words especially challenging to read? Practice reading those again.

HOLIDAY CHALLENGE

Read all the words on line 8 above. All the words on line 8 are from a holiday.
Write the name of that holiday in English here:

____

How many of those are words for things you can eat?

____

PICTURE IT IN HEBREW

Some people enjoy פִּיצָה like this, just topped with cheese.

Other people like vegetables on their פִּיצָה.
It is custom to eat dairy foods, like פִּיצָה on Shavuot.

What other dairy foods do you like to eat?

NEW LETTER פּ

PIZZA – פִּיצָה

THE פֶּסַח SEDER

Read aloud each Hebrew word and its English meaning. Read each sentence describing a פֶּסַח food. Write the correct word to answer each question.

מָרוֹר	מַצָּה	חֲרוֹסֶת	כַּרְפַּס	יַיִן
bitter herbs	matzah	chopped apples and nuts, *charoset*	greens	wine

1 Everyone was in a hurry to leave Egypt and did not have time to wait for the bread dough to rise. My dough hardened into a flat, crunchy kind of bread.

Who am I? ______________________

2 I am the greens on the seder plate. I represent springtime and new life. I am dipped into salt water to remind us of the tears we cried when we were slaves.

Who am I? ______________________

3 I taste bitter. I am a reminder of our bitter lives as slaves.

Who am I? ______________________

4 I remind everyone of the bricks we had to make when we were slaves in Egypt.

Who am I? ______________________

5 I am a sweet liquid. I am poured into a glass four times during the seder. Each time reminds us of God's four promises to bring us from slavery to freedom.

Who am I? ______________________

LESSON 18

שׁוֹפָר

Shofar

LETTERS YOU KNOW. Say the name and sound of each letter.

בּ ת תּ שׁ מ ל כּ ה ר כ ב

ד א ו ק צ ע נ ן ח י ם

ט פּ ס

VOWELS YOU KNOW. Say the sound of each vowel.

NEW LETTER

פ

1	פִי	פֶ	פַ	פוֹ	פְ	פֹ
2	פֶ	פֶּ	פ	פּ	פֹ	פֹּ
3	נָפַ	אֹפֶ	שֶׁפַ	לִפְ	תְּפִ	צוֹפִ

FAY

SHAPE IT UP

What does ***Fay*** look like?
Close your eyes and picture the letter.
Draw it in the air or use your whole body to make the shape of the letter ***Fay***.

Make up a clue to remember ***Fay***

HEADS UP!

The letters פּ and פ make different sounds.

What sound does פּ make?
What sound does פ make?
How do they look different?

Make up a clue to help you remember the difference between פּ and פ.

READY, SET, READ

Read lines 1-4 in a soft voice. Read lines 5-8 in a regular voice.

1 יָפֶה עָפָר כְּפִי נֶפֶשׁ חֹפֶשׁ צוֹפֶה

2 אֹפִי תָּפַס נָפַל אָפָה יָפִים נַפְשִׁי

3 אֹפֶן אֶפֶס צָפוֹן שֶׁפַע כֹּפֶר יִפְתֶּה

4 אָסַפְתָּ אֶפְשָׁר תְּפִלָּה מַפְטִיר תִּפְתַּח לִפְעָמִים

5 תְּפִלּוֹת סְפָרִים סוֹפְרִים לְפָנִים צוֹפִיָּה אַפְקִיד

6 לִפְדּוֹת נוֹפְלִים טוֹטָפֹת נַפְשְׁכֶם תִּפְאֶרֶת

7 אֲפִיקוֹמָן הַפְטָרָה שׁוֹפְטִים כְּמִפְעָלוֹ תְּפִילִין

8 שׁוֹפָר תְּפִלָּה תְּפִילִין מַפְטִיר הַפְטָרָה

I KNOW HEBREW!

Can you find these Hebrew words above?

prayer = תְּפִלָּה

Haftarah = הַפְטָרָה

shofar = שׁוֹפָר

soul = נֶפֶשׁ

afikoman = אֲפִיקוֹמָן

Read and circle or highlight them.

STRIKE A POSE

Show off your best שׁוֹפָר blowing stance!

Make the sound of a שׁוֹפָר too (if it's OK with everyone else in the room).

PICTURE IT IN HEBREW

There's an old Jewish saying that "A good סֵפֶר is like a garden you carry in your hand."

It means that when you read a good סֵפֶר, you feel as if you have traveled to a special place and grown from the experience.

What סֵפֶר have you read that made you feel as if you've traveled somewhere special?

NEW LETTER פ

BOOK – סֵפֶר

PICTURE PERFECT

Read each word aloud. Match the correct word with its picture.

טַלִּית

תּוֹרָה

שׁוֹפָר

פֶּסַח

אֲרוֹן הַקֹּדֶשׁ

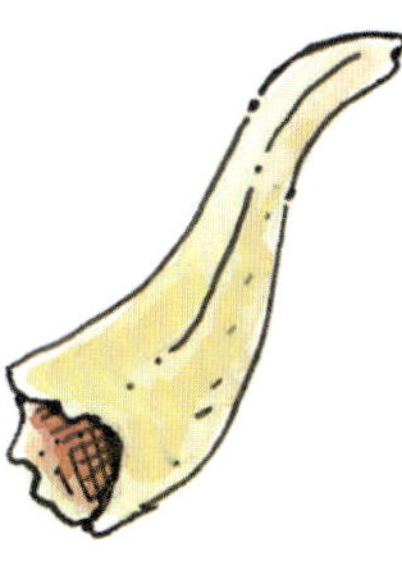

Tree of Life

LETTERS YOU KNOW. Say the name and sound of each letter.

בּ ת תּ שׁ מ ל כּ ה ר כ ב
ד א ו ק צ ע נ ן ח י ם
ט פּ ס פ

VOWELS YOU KNOW. Say the sound of each vowel.

NEW LETTER

ץ

NEW VOWELS

1 שֵׁי פֵּי מֵי לֵי דֵ נֵי

2 פֵּי סֵ טֵי יֵי עֵי כֵּ

3 סֵפֶ כֹּהֵ אוֹמֵ הֵיטֵ דְרֵי שְׁרֵי

Read the lines above. Which Hebrew sound reminds you of a horse?

Circle or highlight it.

SHAPE IT UP

What does ֵ sound like?

Make a hand motion to show the shape of ֵ as you say its sound.

What does ֵי sound like?

Make a hand motion to show the shape of ֵי as you say its sound.

RHYME TIME

Read aloud the words to the right. Circle or highlight the two on each line that rhyme. Sing the rhyming words aloud.

1 בֵּן נֵר תֵּל כֵּן

2 אָמַר אָמֵן שָׁמֵן עֹמֶר

3 קוֹרֵא תּוֹקֵעַ שׁוֹמֵר שׁוֹמֵעַ

4 מִנְיָן מִקְוָה בִּנְיָן בָּנִים

5 טַהֵר טוֹבָה מַהֵר מִצְוָה

6 תִּפְאֶרֶת שַׁחֲרִית אוֹמְרוֹת סוֹפֶרֶת

7 צְדָקָה רַחֲמִים רַחֲמָן צַדִּיקִים

8 מַלְאֲכֵי פְּעָמִים פַּעֲמוֹן פִּרְקֵי

FINAL TZADEE

ץ

1 עֵץ קֵץ חֵץ רָץ אָץ נֵץ

2 עֵץ עֵצִים רָץ רָצָה לֵץ לֵיצָן

3 צֵץ צַע רֶץ פִּיץ רֶן צָה

SHAPE IT UP

What does ***Final Tzadee*** look like?
Close your eyes and picture the letter.
Draw it in the air or use your whole body to make the shape of the letter ***Final Tzadee***.

Make up a clue to remember ***Final Tzadee***.

HEADS UP!

There are five letters in the Hebrew alphabet that have a different form when they come at the end of a word.

When a צ comes at the end of a word, it is a ***Final*** ץ.

Can you name two other letters that have a final form?

READY, SET, READ

Read aloud the lines below. Then read again only the words that end with a ***Final Tzadee***.

1	אֶרֶץ	חָמֵץ	מַצָּה	חָפֵץ	קַיִץ	אֹמֶץ
2	קוֹץ	קוֹצִים	בּוֹץ	פָּרַץ	קוֹפֵץ	קוֹפֶצֶת
3	נוֹצֵץ	לוֹחֵץ	צַנְחָן	עָצִיץ	מִיץ	נִמְצַץ
4	אִמֵּץ	אֶמְצַע	מֶרֶץ	אָמִיץ	הֵצִיץ	צִיֵּן
5	לִקְפֹּץ	קְפִיצָה	קָמָץ	חוֹלֵץ	חוֹלֵם	הֵפִיץ
6	רוֹחֵץ	רָחֲצָה	יוֹעֵץ	צִפֹּרֶן	וֶאֱמַץ	פֶּרֶץ
7	לְשַׁבֵּץ	נִצְטַוָּה	מֵלִיץ	צְבָעִים	צָפוֹן	חָמִיץ

8 עֵץ חַיִּים   הַמּוֹצִיא לֶחֶם מִן הָאָרֶץ

Great job!

I KNOW HEBREW!

Can you find these Hebrew words above?

Tree of Life = עֵץ חַיִּים

leavened food = חָמֵץ

Read and circle or highlight them.

Can you find the Hebrew word for the special food we eat during פֶּסַח?

What line is it on? ______.

Does that word contain a ***Tzadee*** or a ***Final Tzadee***?

PICTURE IT IN HEBREW

An עֵץ, like a person, can be young or old, tall or short. An עֵץ can grow fruit and gives us shade on a sunny day. Many small animals call an עֵץ their home. This עֵץ in Israel grows sweet oranges.

What kind of עֵץ do you like?

NEW LETTER ץ

TREE – עֵץ

CONNECTIONS

Connect the beginning of a phrase with its ending. Say the phrase out loud.

1	הַמּוֹצִיא	נִשְׁתַּנָּה
2	מַה	תּוֹרָה
3	עֵץ	מִצְרָיִם
4	סֵפֶר	לֶחֶם
5	יְצִיאַת	חַיִּים

6	יוֹם	עֲלֵיכֶם
7	אֲרוֹן	טוֹבָה
8	נֵר	הַקֹּדֶשׁ
9	שָׁנָה	תָּמִיד
10	שָׁלוֹם	טוֹב

ALEF BET CHART

You have learned 5 new letters in Lessons 15-19:

ץ פ ס פּ ט

Turn to the ***Alef Bet*** chart on page 96. Color in the new letters.

Can you say the name and sound of each letter you now know?

LESSON 20

יִשְׂרָאֵל

Israel

LETTERS YOU KNOW. Say the name and sound of each letter.

בּ ת תּ שׁ מ ל כּ ה ר כ ב

ד א ו ק צ ע נ ן ח י ם

ט פּ ס פ ץ

VOWELS YOU KNOW. Say the sound of each vowel.

◌ַ ◌ָ ◌ְ ◌ֲ ◌ִ ◌ִי ◌וֹ

◌ֹ ◌ֶ ◌ֱ ◌ֵ ◌ֵי

NEW LETTER

SIN

1 שָׂ שִׂי שֵׂי שׂוֹ שֶׂ שֵׂ

2 שֵׂ שֵׂ שִׂי שִׂי שׂוֹ שׂוֹ

3 מַשָׂ שָׂשׂוֹ שֶׂבַ שָׂפָ יִשָׂ עֶשְׂ

SHAPE IT UP

What does ***Sin*** look like?

Close your eyes and picture the letter.

Draw it in the air or use your whole body to make the shape of the letter ***Sin***.

Make up a clue to remember ***Sin***.

HEADS UP!

The letters שׁ and שׂ make different sounds.

What sound does שׁ make?

What sound does שׂ make?

How do they look different?

Make up a clue to help you remember the difference between שׁ and שׂ.

READY, SET, READ

Read aloud all the words that start with ***Sin***. Next, read all the words that have a ***Sin*** in the middle of the word. Then, read all the words that do not have a ***Sin***.

1	שֶׂה	שִׂים	שַׂר	שָׂם	שַׂק	שִׂיא
2	שָׂרָה	שָׂנֵא	שָׂמַח	עֶשֶׂר	עֹשֶׂה	מַשָׂא
3	שָׂרָה	שָׂרָה	שָׂמָה	שָׂמָה	שַׂעַר	שָׂשׂוֹן
4	שֵׂעָר	שָׂכָר	שָׂפָה	יִשָׂא	בָּשָׂר	שֵׂכֶל
5	שָׂדֶה	פָּשַׂט	שֶׂבַע	עֶשֶׂר	עָשָׂה	תַּיִשׁ
6	שִׂמְחַת	תּוֹרָה	שְׁמוֹנֶה	עֶשְׂרֵה	עֲשֶׂרֶת	הַדִּבְּרוֹת
7	שְׁמַע	יִשְׂרָאֵל	שִׂים	שָׁלוֹם	עוֹשֶׂה	שָׁלוֹם
8	עַם	יִשְׂרָאֵל	בְּנֵי	יִשְׂרָאֵל	אֶרֶץ	יִשְׂרָאֵל

I KNOW HEBREW!

Can you find the Hebrew words above?

Ten Commandments = עֲשֶׂרֶת הַדִּבְּרוֹת

Rejoicing of the Torah = שִׂמְחַת תּוֹרָה

Israel = יִשְׂרָאֵל

WORD RIDDLE

I am a holiday we celebrate each year when we finish reading the entire תּוֹרָה.

We then begin reading the תּוֹרָה from the very first word all over again.

My name begins with שׂ. What holiday am I?

PICTURE IT IN HEBREW

A family celebration such as a wedding, baby naming or b'nai mitzvah is called a שִׂמְחָה.

When you bring שִׂמְחָה to someone's life, you bring שִׂמְחָה to yourself too.

Think about how you recently brought שִׂמְחָה to someone's life.

TOURING יִשְׂרָאֵל

Below are the names of eight places in יִשְׂרָאֵל.

Read aloud the Hebrew name of each place.

Then look at the map of יִשְׂרָאֵל.

Write or say the matching number for each English name.

1 צְפַת

2 תֵּל-אָבִיב

3 אֵילַת

4 הֶרְצְלִיָּה

5 מְצָדָה

6 חֵיפָה

7 יְרוּשָׁלַיִם

8 בְּאֵר שֶׁבַע

LESSON 21

חַג שָׂמֵחַ

Happy Holiday

LETTERS YOU KNOW. Say the name and sound of each letter.

בּ ת תּ שׁ מ ל כּ ה ר כ ב

ד א ו ק צ ע נ ן ח י ם

ט פּ ס פ ץ שׂ

VOWELS YOU KNOW. Say the sound of each vowel.

◌ַ ◌ָ ◌ְ ◌ֲ ◌ִ ◌ִי ◌וֹ

◌ֹ ◌ֶ ◌ֱ ◌ֵ ◌ֵי

NEW LETTER

ג

GIMMEL

1 גַ גוֹ גִי גֶ גַ גֵי

2 גַג גַלוֹ גַבֵּי גַנֵי גִיס גִיר

3 גֶד גִבּוֹ גָאַ הָג גִטִי גוֹלָ

SHAPE IT UP

What does ***Gimmel*** look like?

Close your eyes and picture the letter.

Draw it in the air or use your whole body to make the shape of the letter ***Gimmel***.

Make up a clue to remember ***Gimmel***.

RHYME TIME

Read the Hebrew words below. Connect the rhyming words, then sing them out loud.

1	רֶגֶל	הַגָּדָה
2	מָשִׁיחַ	סוֹלֵחַ
3	אַגָּדָה	דֶּגֶל
4	פּוֹקֵחַ	שָׁלִיחַ

5	כֹּחַ	גוֹמֵל
6	יָרֵחַ	טָהוֹר
7	גוֹלֵל	שָׂמֵחַ
8	גִּבּוֹר	מֹחַ

HEADS UP!

When חַ comes at the end of a word, we read the vowel first and then the letter. שָׂמֵחַ sounds like שָׂמֵאַח.

1	כֹּחַ	מֹחַ	רֵיחַ	נֹחַ	שִׂיחַ	אֹחַ
2	יָרֵחַ	בַּכֹּחַ	הַמֹּחַ	לְנֹחַ	כְּשִׂיחַ	טִיחַ
3	רֵחַ	מִיחַ	שִׂיחַ	גִּיחַ	רֹחַ	נוֹחַ

READY, SET, READ

The first word on line 1, שָׂמֵחַ, means "happy." Read lines 1-4 in a happy voice. Read lines 5-8 in your regular voice, except when you come to the word שָׂמֵחַ. Read that word in a happy voice.

1 שָׂמֵחַ יָרֵחַ אוֹרֵחַ נָשִׂיחַ מֵנִיחַ בַּכֹּחַ

2 מָשִׁיחַ פּוֹקֵחַ סוֹלֵחַ פּוֹתֵחַ פָּתַח לִפְתֹּחַ

3 לְשַׁבֵּחַ מְנַצֵּחַ שׁוֹלֵחַ מָנוֹחַ שָׁלִיחַ מַפְתֵּחַ

4 מַצְמִיחַ מִשְׁלוֹחַ הִצְלִיחַ לוֹקֵחַ לְשַׂמֵּחַ פּוֹרֵחַ

5 מַשְׁגִּיחַ הַשְׁגָּחָה אָשִׂיחַ שִׂיחָה מְשַׂמֵּחַ שָׂמַח

6 הִבְטִיחַ בָּטַח טוֹרֵחַ טָרַח פִּקֵּחַ נִפְקַח

7 בּוֹרֵחַ לִבְרֹחַ בָּרַח לִסְלֹחַ סָלַח סְלִיחָה

8 מָשִׁיחַ חַג שָׂמֵחַ פֶּסַח הַגָּדָה מְגִלָּה

I KNOW HEBREW!

Can you find the Hebrew words above?

happy holiday = חַג שָׂמֵחַ

moon = יָרֵחַ

Read and circle or highlight them.

PICTURE IT IN HEBREW

A גָמָל can travel great distances across hot, dry deserts with little food or water.

The גָמָל walks easily on soft sand and carries people and heavy loads to places that have no roads.

What do you think is in the hump of the גָמָל?

NEW LETTER ג

CAMEL – גָמָל

I HAVE A LITTLE DREIDEL

Add the ending sound חַ to complete the word on the driedles. Read the words to a classsmate.

קִדּוּשׁ

Kiddush

LETTERS YOU KNOW. Say the name and sound of each letter.

בּ ת תּ שׁ מ ל כּ ה ר כ ב

ד א ו ק צ ע נ ן ח י ם

ט פּ ס פ ץ שׂ ג

VOWELS YOU KNOW. Say the sound of each vowel.

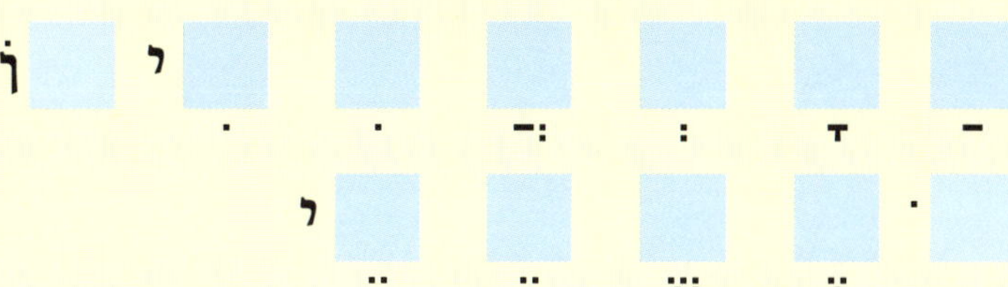

NEW VOWEL

וּ ֻ

1 סוּ שׂוּ טוּ נוּ מוּ צוּ

2 בֻּ גֻ שֻׁ רֻ קֻ תֻּ

3 הוּא לָנוּ אָנוּ בָּנוּ צוּד כֻּלוֹ

SHAPE IT UP

What does וּ sound like?

Make a hand motion to show the shape of וּ as you say its sound.

What does ֻ sound like?

Make a hand motion to show the shape of ֻ as you say its sound.

What is the sound a cow makes? Circle or highlight it above.

What sound is the opposite of "old"? Circle or highlight it above.

READY, SET, READ

Read aloud the lines below. Point to your belly when you read an "oo" vowel sound.

1	חֻמָּשׁ	לוּחַ	כֻּלָּם	וְהָיוּ	סֻכָּה	טֹבוּ
2	עָלֵינוּ	לִבֵּנוּ	סֻכּוֹת	שָׁבוּעַ	חֲנֻכָּה	קִבּוּץ
3	קִדּוּשׁ	שֻׁלְחָן	מְשֻׁבָּח	סִדּוּר	מְצֻיָּן	כֻּלָּנוּ
4	הַלְלוּיָה	גְּדֻלָּה	פָּסוּק	יְשׁוּעָה	נְטוּיָה	אֲנַחְנוּ
5	וּבְנֻחֹה	לוּלָב	וְיָפֻצוּ	וַיְכֻלּוּ	וְיָנֻסוּ	דַּיֵּנוּ
6	תְּמוּנָה	וְצִוָּנוּ	אֵלִיָּהוּ	הַנָּבִיא	בָּרְכוּ	קֻשְׁיוֹת
7	קְדֻשָּׁה	יְהוּדִים	פּוּרִים	יוֹם	כִּפּוּר	שָׁבוּעוֹת
8	יְרוּשָׁלַיִם	אֱלֹהֵינוּ	שֶׁהֶחֱיָנוּ	אָבִינוּ	מַלְכֵּנוּ	

I KNOW HEBREW!

Can you find these Hebrew words above?

The Five Books of Moses = חֻמָּשׁ

Jerusalem = יְרוּשָׁלַיִם

Elijah the Prophet = אֵלִיָּהוּ הַנָּבִיא

Kiddush = קִדּוּשׁ

prayer book = סִדּוּר

Jews = יְהוּדִים

Read and circle or highlight them.

EXTRA CREDIT

Can you find the Hebrew word for ***prayer book*** in the lines above?

Underline the word.

I SPY

Read aloud each line.

Find the Hebrew that sounds the same as the English in the box. Circle it or highlight it.

1	SHOO	שְׁ	שׁוּ	שׁוֹ	שִׁי	שֶׁ	שֵׁי
2	FOH	פוּ	פָ	פוֹ	פִ	פְ	פֵי
3	AH	עֹ	עֶ	עִ	עֶ	עֲ	עוּ
4	SEE	שָׂ	שֶׂ	שֶׂ	שׂוֹ	שַׂ	שִׂי
5	YOH	יוּ	יֹ	יָ	יִי	יֵי	יֶ
6	PEH	פֶּ	פְּ	פַּ	פֶּ	פּוֹ	פֵּי
7	TSOO	צֵי	צְ	צוּ	צָ	צִ	צֹ
8	SOO	סַ	סוֹ	סֶ	סִי	סְ	סֵ
9	EH	אִי	אוּ	אָ	אֶ	אֱ	אֹ
10	TAY	טוֹ	טַ	טֶ	טֵי	טִ	טֹ

POWER READING

Practice reading these prayer phrases from the קִדּוּשׁ, which we recite over wine.

Write the number of words with the vowel וּ you find on each line.

1	____	אֲשֶׁר קִדְּשָׁנוּ בְּמִצְווֹתָיו וְרָצָה בָנוּ
2	____	וְשַׁבָּת...בְּאַהֲבָה וּבְרָצוֹן הִנְחִילָנוּ
3	____	כִּי הוּא יוֹם תְּחִלָּה לְמִקְרָאֵי קֹדֶשׁ
4	____	כִּי בָנוּ בָחַרְתָּ וְאוֹתָנוּ קִדַּשְׁתָּ
5	____	בְּאַהֲבָה וּבְרָצוֹן הִנְחַלְתָּנוּ
6	____	מְקַדֵּשׁ הַשַּׁבָּת

PICTURE IT IN HEBREW

How would you like to eat a קַקְטוּס? A קַקְטוּס plant is covered with prickly spines, but if you are careful, you can use some kinds of קַקְטוּס for food.

Jams and sweets are made from קַקְטוּס fruits and their juicy stems. The pricky-pear קַקְטוּס in this photo is called a sabra and grows in Israel.

Have you ever seen a real קַקְטוּס?

NEW VOWEL ְ

CACTUS – קַקְטוּס

HOLIDAY QUIZ

Use the Hebrew names of each holiday on the right to answer the questions. Draw a line connecting each question to its answer.

1	We read the מְגִלָּה. What holiday am I?	יוֹם כִּפּוּר
2	We shake the ***lulav*** and eat in a small booth. What holiday am I?	פּוּרִים
3	We celebrate the giving of the Torah. What holiday am I?	סֻכּוֹת
4	We light the ***hanukkiyah***. What holiday am I?	שָׁבוּעוֹת
5	We do not eat all day. What holiday am I?	חֲנֻכָּה

מְזוּזָה

Mezuzah

LETTERS YOU KNOW. Say the name and sound of each letter.

בּ ת תּ שׁ מ ל כּ ה ר כ ב

ד א ו ק צ ע נ ן ח י ם

ט פּ ס פ ץ שׂ ג

VOWELS YOU KNOW. Say the sound of each vowel.

◌ַ ◌ָ ◌ְ ◌ֲ ◌ִ ◌ִי ◌וֹ

◌ֹ ◌ֶ ◌ֱ ◌ֵ ◌ֵי ◌וּ ◌ֻ

NEW LETTER

ז

ZAYIN

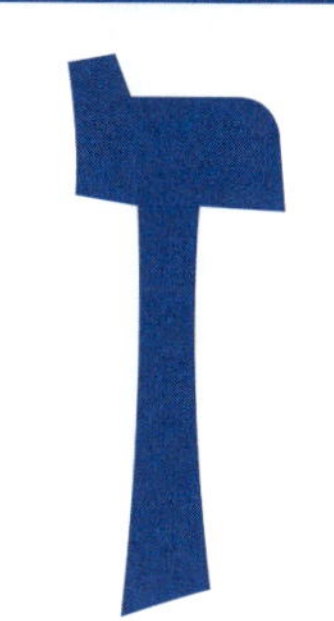

1	זֻ	זוּ	זוֹ	זִ	זְ	זֵי
2	זֶ	שֶׂ	זַ	סַ	זִ	צִ
3	חַז	זָוִי	זַךְ	יִזְ	זֶן	זוֹר

Which Hebrew sound reminds you of a place to see lots of animals?

SHAPE IT UP

What does *Zayin* look like?

Close your eyes and picture the letter.

Draw it in the air or use your whole body to make the shape of the letter *Zayin*.

HEADS UP!

The Hebrew letters ז, ס, צ, and שׂ make similar sounds.

What sound does each letter make?

Read each word carefully.

זְמַן חֶסֶד מִצְוָה שִׂמְחָה

READY, SET, READ

Read aloud all the words that start with a ***Zayin***. Then read all the words that end with a ***Zayin***. Are there words left? Read those too.

1	זֶה	אָז	עֹז	פָּז	בּוּז	זָר
2	זָכֹר	זְמַן	אֹזֶן	חָזָק	חַזָן	אָחַז
3	הַזָן	זֶבַח	זֹאת	מַזָל	זָקֵן	זָהָב
4	יִזְכֹּר	מָעוֹז	זֵכֶר	אֵיזֶה	עֶזֵנוּ	וְזַרְעוֹ
5	זִכָּרוֹן	מִזְבֵּחַ	מַחְזוֹר	מִזְמוֹר	נֶעֱזָב	זָוִית
6	זְכוּת	מִזְרָח	זְרוֹעַ	מָזוֹן	זַרְעָם	עִזִים
7	זַיִת	הֶחֱזִיר	זָקוּק	הִזְנִיחַ	חֲזַק	וֶאֱמַץ
8	מְזוּזָה	יוֹם	הַזִכָּרוֹן	מַחֲזוֹר	מַזָל	טוֹב

Say מַזָל טוֹב! That means "congratulations"!

I KNOW HEBREW!

Can you find these Hebrew words above?

mezuzah = מְזוּזָה

mahzor = מַחֲזוֹר

Read and circle or highlight them.

PRAYER PRACTICE

Practice reading these siddur phrases. Look for ***Zayin***s as you read. Write the number of words that have a ***Zayin*** on each line.

1 ____ הַזָּן אֶת הַכֹּל

2 ____ זִכָּרוֹן לְמַעֲשֵׂה בְרֵאשִׁית

3 ____ זֵכֶר לִיצִיאַת מִצְרָיִם

4 ____ עֵץ חַיִּים הִיא לַמַּחֲזִיקִים בָּה

5 ____ וְלוֹ הָעֹז וְהַמִּשְׂרָה

6 ____ אָז אֶגְמֹר בְּשִׁיר מִזְמוֹר

7 ____ וּכְתַבְתָּם עַל מְזֻזוֹת

8 ____ עוֹזֵר וּמוֹשִׁיעַ וּמָגֵן

9 ____ בַּיָּמִים הָהֵם בַּזְּמַן הַזֶּה

10 ____ שֶׁהֶחֱיָנוּ וְקִיְּמָנוּ וְהִגִּיעָנוּ לַזְּמַן הַזֶּה

I SPY

Read aloud the Hebrew words on each line. Circle or highlight the letter in each word that sounds like the English in the box.

1	S	פּוֹרֵשׁ	יִשְׂרָאֵל	שֵׂכֶל	שִׂמְחָה
2	Z	יִזְכֹּר	מַזָּל	זוֹרֵחַ	גְּזֵרָה
3	ACH	מָשִׁיחַ	הִצְלִיחַ	לַמְנַצֵּחַ	מִזְבֵּחַ
4	G	גְּמָרָא	הַגָּדָה	מְגִלָּה	גֶּשֶׁם
5	TS	אֶרֶץ	חָמֵץ	וֶאֱמַץ	קִבּוּץ
6	V	זַיִן	זוּג	וְזֹאת	וְזַרְעוֹ

PICTURE IT IN HEBREW

Jerusalem is often called "the city of זָהָב."

One reason is because of the gleaming dome of זָהָב on this mosque, which was built in the seventh century.

At sunset, the stone buildings throughout Jerusalem look as if they glow זָהָב too.

GOLD – זָהָב

NAME TAG

Read the name of each letter in the box. Find its matching Hebrew letter and circle it. What sound does the letter make?

בּ	ס	פּ	תּ	כּ	PAY	1
ע	שׁ	צ	שׂ	ל	SIN	2
ן	ד	נ	ו	ג	GIMMEL	3
פ	בּ	ת	כ	פּ	FAY	4
ק	שׂ	ס	צ	ם	SAMECH	5

DOUBLE MEANING

9=ט	8=ח	7=ז	6=ו	5=ה	4=ד	3=ג	2=בּ	1=א
90=צ	80=פּ	70=ע	60=ס	50=נ	40=מ	30=ל	20=כּ	10=י
400=ת	300=ש	200=ר	100=ק					

The word "life"/ חַי is equal to the number 18 (8 ח + 10 י).
This is considered a good luck number in Jewish tradition.

בָּרוּךְ

Praised, Blessed

NEW LETTER

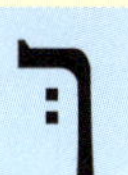

LETTERS YOU KNOW. Say the name and sound of each letter.

בּ ת תּ שׁ מ ל כּ ה ר כ ב

ד א ו ק צ ע נ ן ח י ם

ט פּ ס פ ץ שׂ ג ז

VOWELS YOU KNOW. Say the sound of each vowel.

◌ַ ◌ָ ◌ְ ◌ֲ ◌ִ ◌ִי ◌וֹ

◌ֹ ◌ֶ ◌ֱ ◌ֵ ◌ֵי וּ ◌ֻ

FINAL CHAF

1 רַךְ כַּךְ בָּךְ לֵךְ לְךָ וּלְךָ

2 אַךְ בְּךָ שֶׁלְךָ בְּכָךְ שִׁמְךָ תֶיךָ

SHAPE IT UP

What does ***Final Chaf*** look like?

Close your eyes and picture the letter.

Draw it in the air or use your whole body to make the shape of the letter ***Final Chaf***.

Make up a clue to remember ***Final Chaf***.

HEADS UP!

Final ך is the only final letter that always has a vowel. Read these words.

הַמְבֹרָךְ בֵּיתֶךָ

READING RULE When  comes at the end of a word, the י is silent.

READY, SET, READ

Read aloud each word that ends with a vowel sound ךָ.
Then read aloud each word that ends with ךְ.

1 בָּרוּךְ אִמֶּךָ שְׁמֵךְ עַמְּךָ דֶּרֶךְ עָלֶיךָ

2 מֶלֶךְ לִבְּךָ רֵעֲךָ פֶּרֶךְ אֶרֶךְ לִבֵּךְ

3 כָּמוֹךָ צָרִיךְ הוֹלֵךְ אֵלֶיךָ אָבִיךָ עֻזֶּךָ

4 בָּרוּךְ בָּנֶיךָ עִמְּךָ בֵּיתֶךָ אוֹתְךָ כֻּלְּךָ

5 מְבֹרָךְ יִמְלֹךְ לְבָבְךָ יָדֶיךָ מְאֹדֶךָ חֻקֶּיךָ

6 לְפָנֶיךָ עֵינֶיךָ נַפְשְׁךָ מְצַוְּךָ סוֹמֵךְ מַלְאָךְ

7 בָּרוּךְ קֻדֶּשָׁתְךָ בִּשְׁלוֹמֶךָ אֱלֹהַיִךְ וַיְבָרֶךְ

8 תַּנַּךְ מִצְוֹתֶיךָ וּבְלֶכְתְּךָ וּבְקוּמֶךָ וּבִשְׁעָרֶיךָ

I KNOW HEBREW!

Can you find these Hebrew words above?

praised, blessed = בָּרוּךְ

king, ruler = מֶלֶךְ

Read and circle or highlight them.

EXTRA CREDIT

Perhaps you've heard a song about a מֶלֶךְ named דָּוִד.

Can you sing the song and/or do the hand motions that go along with it?

Ask a partner to do it with you!

PICTURE IT IN HEBREW

Looking at this דֶּרֶךְ, you can see there is a choice about which way to go. דֶּרֶךְ also means "way"—the way you choose to live. The phrase דֶּרֶךְ אֶרֶץ, literally "the way of the land," means having good manners and showing respect to people and the world around you.

How do you choose which way to go?

NEW LETTER ךְ

ROAD – דֶּרֶךְ

בָּרוּךְ אַתָּה, יְיָ אֱלֹהֵינוּ, מֶלֶךְ הָעוֹלָם...

Praised are you, Adonai our God, Ruler of the world....

who brings forth bread from the earth.	הַמּוֹצִיא לֶחֶם מִן הָאָרֶץ.	1
who creates the fruit of the vine.	בּוֹרֵא פְּרִי הַגָּפֶן.	2
who creates the fruit of the earth.	בּוֹרֵא פְּרִי הָאֲדָמָה.	3
who creates the fruit of the tree.	בּוֹרֵא פְּרִי הָעֵץ.	4
who creates many kinds of food.	בּוֹרֵא מִינֵי מְזוֹנוֹת.	5
by whose word all things come into being.	שֶׁהַכֹּל נִהְיֶה בִּדְבָרוֹ.	6
for keeping us in life, for sustaining us, and for helping us to reach this day.	שֶׁהֶחֱיָנוּ וְקִיְּמָנוּ וְהִגִּיעָנוּ לַזְּמַן הַזֶּה.	7

SHOW WHAT YOU KNOW

Put a ★ next to the blessing you would say over חַלָּה.

Put a ✔ next to the blessing you would say over wine or grape juice.

List three foods for which would you use the blessing that ends "who creates the fruit of the earth." Draw them here:

LESSON 25

אָלֶף

Alef

NEW LETTER

ף

LETTERS YOU KNOW. Say the name and sound of each letter.

בּ ת תּ שׁ מ ל כּ ה ר כ ב

ד א ו ק צ ע נ ן ח י ם

ט פּ ס פ ץ שׂ ג ז ך

VOWELS YOU KNOW. Say the sound of each vowel.

◌ַ ◌ָ ◌ְ ◌ֲ ◌ִ ◌ִי ◌וֹ

◌ֹ ◌ֶ ◌ֱ ◌ֵ ◌ֵי ◌וּ ◌ֻ

1	אַף	דַף	עוֹף	קוֹף	גוּף	סוּף
2	כַּף	תּוֹף	עָף	סוֹף	תַּף	כֵּף
3	יֵף	נָף	טֶף	סָף	רַף	צוּף

SHAPE IT UP

What does ***Final Fay*** look like?

Close your eyes and picture the letter.

Draw it in the air or use your whole body to make the shape of the letter ***Final Fay***.

Make up a clue to remember ***Final Fay***.

HEADS UP!

When a פ comes at the end of a word, it is a ***Final*** ף.

There are five letters in the Hebrew alphabet that have a different form when they come at the end of a word.

Name the other four letters that have a final form.

READY, SET, READ

The letter ***Final Fay*** makes the sound of the English letter ***F***. Read lines 1-3 to a **f**riend in a **f**unny voice. Read lines 4-6 in a **f**rightened voice. Read lines 7-8 in a **f**ancy voice.

1 נוֹף הַדַף חַף עָיֵף סַף חוֹף

2 חֹרֶף תֵּיכֶף עֹרֶף עָנָף כֶּסֶף שָׂרַף

3 שֶׁטֶף יוֹסֵף אֶלֶף חָלַף כָּתֵף כָּפַף

4 מוּסָף צָפוּף קְלַף זוֹקֵף קוֹטֵף לָעוּף

5 אָסַף נִשְׂרַף שִׁטוּף רָצוּף כָּנָף יָחֵף

6 עַפְעַף מְרַחֵף רוֹדֵף שָׁלוֹם זוֹקֵף כְּפוּפִים

7 מְצַפְצֵף לְהִתְאַסֵף לֶאֱסֹף הֶחֱלִיף לְשַׁפְשֵׁף

8 אָלֶף בֵּית וְצִוָּנוּ לְהִתְעַטֵף בַּצִיצִית

I KNOW HEBREW!

Can you find these Hebrew words above?

alef = אָלֶף

alef bet = אָלֶף בֵּית

Read and circle or highlight them.

EXTRA CREDIT

Can you find the Hebrew name for Joseph in the lines above? (Hint: The Hebrew name for Joseph begins with the letter ***Yud***.)

Tell a partner what you know about the story of Joseph, the son of יַעֲקֹב and רָחֵל.

Can you find the Hebrew word for peace in the lines above? Circle or highlight it.

READING RELAY

In column א, Player 1 reads word 1. Player 2 reads words 1 and 2. Player 3 reads words 1, 2, and 3. Continue the relay until all ten words in the column have been read. Then repeat the Reading Relay with the words in columns ב and ג.

	א		ב		ג
	פּ		פּ פ		ף
1	פָּסוּק	11	אֲפִיקוֹמָן	21	כָּנָף
2	פּוֹקֵחַ	12	שׁוֹפָר	22	אָלֶף
3	פֻּרְקָן	13	גֶּפֶן	23	קֶלַף
4	פְּעָמִים	14	סֵפֶר	24	יוֹסֵף
5	פָּרָשָׁה	15	תְּפִלָּה	25	רוֹדֵף
6	פּוּרִים	16	מַפְטִיר	26	מְרַחֵף
7	פֶּסַח	17	תְּפִילִין	27	מוּסָף
8	פְּרִי	18	לִפְנֵי	28	זוֹקֵף
9	פֶּרֶךְ	19	מִשְׁפָּחָה	29	תֵּיכֶף
10	פָּנִים	20	תַּפּוּחַ	30	אָסַף

EXTRA CREDIT

Can you find the Hebrew word for ***afikoman***? Circle or highlight it above.

Can you find the Hebrew word for ***Passover***? Circle or highlight it above.

PICTURE IT IN HEBREW

Your אַף is very useful. You can use your אַף to smell good things, like flowers or yummy food.

Hold your אַף closed while you try to speak, and you'll discover another job of your אַף! It affects your tone of voice and the ways the letters sound.

Can you think of another thing your אַף does?

NEW LETTER ף

NOSE – אַף

I SPY

Read each line. Circle or highlight the Hebrew letters that sound the same as the English in the box.

1	CH	סוֹמֵךְ	לְפָנֶיךָ	תְּפִילִין	מַלְכוּתְךָ
2	CH	כְּבוֹד	בְּתוֹכֵנוּ	כָּמֹכָה	זוֹכֵר
3	F	מַפְטִיר	תְּפִלָּה	פָּנִים	אֲפִיקוֹמָן
4	F	רוֹדֵף	בָּרוּךְ	מוּסָף	זוֹקֵף
5	M	נוֹפְלִים	כְּפוּפִים	מְפַרְנֵס	הִתְפַּלֵּל
6	M	מַצּוֹת	מִשְׁפָּטִים	שְׁמוֹ	טוּבוֹ

ALEF BET CHART

You have learned five new letters in Lessons 20-25.

שׂ ג ז ץ ף

Turn to the אָלֶף בֵּית chart on page 96. Color in the new letters.

מַזָל טוֹב! You have learned every letter in the אָלֶף בֵּית. Recite the complete אָלֶף בֵּית.

Give yourself a pat on the back. . . you deserve it!!

אָלֶף בֵּית

ALEF
BET
VET
GIMMEL
DALET
HEY
VAV
ZAYIN
CHET
TET
YUD
KAF
CHAF
FINAL CHAF
LAMED
MEM
FINAL MEM
NUN
FINAL NUN
SAMECH
AYIN
PAY
FAY
FINAL FAY
TZADEE
FINAL TZADEE
KOOF
RESH
SHIN
SIN
TAV
TAV